Demon's Embrace

Book one of The Redemption of the Fallen

By Scarlett J Rose

ISBN-10:0-9925993-2-6

ISBN-13:978-0-9925993-2-4

Edited by Mirren Hogan

Revised Edition Edited by Susan Horsnell.

Published by Far Horizons Publishing

info.far.horizons@gmail.com

<u>**More by Scarlett J Rose:**</u>

Heart of a Scorpion

Zara's Bond

Tess

Night of the Demon Anthology (The Demon King's
Prize)

<u>**Also in this series Coming Soon:**</u>

Angel's Redemption (Book Two)\

The Demon's Bargain (Book Three)

The Demon's Muse (Book Four)

The Demon's Escape (Book Five)

Thank-You:

To all my fantastic friends who have helped me to get Demon's Embrace and the Fallen Series off the ground.

To my beta readers, Chaira Beltrami Gottmer, Sandy J Cohen and Doug Draa, thank you for your wonderful feedback and loving Decimus and Eve's story as much as I loved writing it.

And to my Editors, Mirren, and Susan Thank you so much for your help with the editing, I'm a grammatical klutz without my editors.

For My Fans.

For your enjoyment of my works brings me pleasure that no Demon can surpass.

Look out for the future books in the Series, Angels Redemption – Thomas' story, The Demon's Bargain, The Demon's Muse and the Demon's Escape.

Thank you all!

-Scarlett J Rose

February 2015

Demon's Embrace

Book one of Redemption of the Fallen.

By Scarlett J Rose

The ground rumbled.

The sky crackled with power as the two armies of Heaven and Hell clashed on Earth. Could this be their final battle?

The hapless people of the world cried out in fright as the two armies came together in bloody battle. Swords and shields clashed, armour swiftly bloodied as Angels with wings of white and Demons displaying black; clashed for supremacy of the souls who dwelled on their battlefield.

Humans witnessing the battle watched in awe and beliefs shattered. On a day free from battle, they would be going about their lives in the cities warmed by the bright yellow sun. Others, were being rudely awoken to the screaming cries of battle.

People ran for their lives, seeking refuge in subways, churches, underground carparks and office buildings. Anywhere that might provide sanctuary from the murderous Demons.

The battle between good and evil was ferocious. Angels, from the heavens above pitted their goodness against the evil Demons of Hell.

A thunderous crash shook the Earth, the ground burst open and a fiery being purged itself from the bowels of Hell. *Hades. Abaddon.* The name of the darkest of Demons was inconsequential compared to his evil.

An answering clarion's call from the heavens above brought forth a brilliant white figure of purity, goodness.

Hades soared, striking at the white figure with such force they were propelled across the sky. Their combined energies flashed, a blinding brilliance that would leave afterimages seared into the eyes of those who were unfortunate enough to witness their ultimate battle rage.

Above the battleground where their armies engaged, evil pulsed with hatred and anger as he fought against the pure white brilliance of love and goodness.

Deafening rumbles echoed throughout the earth. Humans who had failed to find refuge, cowered, mesmerized at the battle playing out above them. Battling Angels and Demons glimpsed the sky as their leaders exchanged vicious blows. The Kings of Heaven and Hell battled to win the souls of every man, woman and child on Earth.

A powerful wave emanated from their point in the sky, power rippled through space and time. Bright light pierced the sky. When the light faded, the sky above was clear. Anguished screams of the lost Angels and Demons below filled the air. Their leaders gone, no longer there to guide them. Their connection with Heaven and Hell lost. Their battle forgotten, Angels and Demons dropped to their knees. Devastation punctuated their faces.

Humans emerged cautiously from their hiding places to utter destruction. The war of Heaven and Hell had wrought havoc on cities and towns. Buildings burned and bodies of humans, Angels and Demons lay scattered amongst the debris.

Confusion reigned the streets as humans attempted to reclaim their world. Unable to return to their realms, Angels were given refuge by churches, Demons were left in a state of mental denial and confusion. No-one willing to give help to such evil.

Over the following days, some Demons refused to acquiesce and continued to fight. Humans were taken as slaves, Angels were slaughtered and cities claimed as their own. Fortunate Demons were taken in by small groups of government entities set up by cities which fared better after the war.

Many of the unfortunate Demons who had survived the war, now roamed with the homeless. Their only hope of survival lay in the Demon rehabilitation programs offered by the governments of the more stable cities.

Chapter One

Six months later.

Eve Macintyre glanced at the clock on the wall of her office in the Demon Rehabilitation Services building. It was barely ten in the morning. She sighed as she checked who her next client was. *Marius, great.* Her mood deteriorated, her day couldn't possibly get any worse. She detested being on the client relations rotation of the roster. Dealing with the displaced Demons who had invaded and almost destroyed the world could be trying, to say the least. She loved her job, she took great pride in helping those in need. Dealing with Demons like Marius, whose temper was as unpredictable and volatile as a volcano, along with a planet-sized chip on his shoulder, was something she hadn't envisaged.

Eve lifted her head as Marius entered her office. No knock, no waiting for an invitation. He wore a permanent scowl on his handsome face, his muscles strained against the tight black tank top. His wings prevented him from walking through the doorway like any normal person. He was forced to ease in sideways while ducking his tall frame under the door jam. His frown deepened as his mood darkened.

Demons for the most part were unusually handsome with muscled, athletic bodies. The only difference between them and athletic humans who sported similar physiques, were the black wings adorning their backs.

Eve stood as Marius stopped before her desk.

"Good morning, Mr. Marius, I hope you are well today?" She extended her hand toward him.

Marius ignored her extended hand, grunted and sat in a chair opposite her.

Eve eyed him warily, and retracted her hand from the tense air between them. She sat and pulled his file from the small pile on her desk. Her computer had yet to be replaced after his last visit. Marius was one of the most volatile of their clientele. Two of the Demons, who had been given a security position within the program, stood outside her door. They were ready to take charge of Marius should the need arise.

"Any luck in your hunt for a job, Mr. Marius?" Eve scanned his file, police reports of assaults and property damage were prevalent. Law officials refused to imprison a

Demon, it was a waste of their resources and time. They simply broke out of prison and liberated a few human prisoners with them.

Marius' hands gripped the edge of her desk, cracking the pressed wood he leaned forward. "I *had* a job. It was to destroy the enemy and capture humans for my Lord to enslave. I was *extremely* good at it." His teeth clenched. "I *will* finish that job one day. One day quite soon and all humans will tremble at *my* feet as their master!"

He glared into Eve's eyes as he leaned closer. "I will have women chained at my throne for my pleasure. Men will die at the hands of my soldiers for my entertainment. Hell will rise again, with me as the greatest dark king of all time."

The crack as the edge of her desk fractured caused Eve to jump in fright. She stood and stepped back as Marius also rose from his seat.

"That's enough, Marius." The shake in her voice indicated her fear. She lifted her hand and backed against the wall, trying to put as much distance between them as she could.

He encroached on her space and leaned close. She shuddered at the lust burning his eyes. "You are pretty. I think I will take you as my first."

He skirted the desk ever closer to her. His eyes alight with dark desire. His wings flexed, feathers as black as the darkest night shivered and fluttered to the ground. His voice was menacing. "You know, Miss Eve, Demons are insatiable lovers, we are able to fuck for hours." His lips grazed her ear, his breath caused her to tremble with fear. "I think you'd like that, to be my sex slave, chained and collared, ready to do my bidding." She turned her head away from him.

Shit. Eve felt the warmth of his body, he refused to retreat.

Marius reached for her. His calloused fingers traced her jawline, she trembled beneath his touch.

"Yes." His eyes flashed, his dark wings trembled excitedly as they folded around her. "You would be my prized slave."

Eve gulped in much needed air. "Security." Her voice was hoarse but, within seconds she heard the thump of feet as her rescuers entered her office.

A slight breeze accompanied the shifting of his ebony wings as the security Demons dragged Marius away. They hauled him from her office, slamming him against the doorframe hard enough to crack the tall pane of glass beside the door.

Eve wrapped her arms around her waist and composed herself. She teetered from her office on unsteady legs. As she attempted to close the door behind her, she noted it didn't quite fit anymore. She heard Marius cursing and shouting as he was dragged from the building. He vowed, one day he would bring his men back together and they would finish what they had started.

She staggered to the staff room, her body trembling. Her hand shook as she reached for a cup from the water cooler. The empty water tank taunted her. She would have to get the much needed water from the client's waiting area, where the only other tank was located. She strode quickly to the room where she found a couple of other Demons waiting. She was grateful for the quiet day and lack of clients. Her hand progressed from trembling to uncontrollable shaking making filling the cup almost impossible. More water decorated the floor than entered the cup.

"Please, allow me to assist you." The voice was deep, soothing. A large, gentle hand reached out and enfolded her trembling hand. The water achieved her goal of filling the cup.

Eve turned and gazed up at one of the most strikingly handsome men no, Demon, she had laid eyes on. His hair was dark, thick and curly. His jaw square and strong but it was his eyes which captured her and held her riveted to him. They the most piercingly blue eyes she had ever encountered and they gazed into her own.

"Th-thank-you." She retrieved the cup and her hand from his deliciously warm touch.

He nodded, his smile tight. She watched as he sat back down, picked up a newspaper and perused the job section. She stood ogling him, wondering where he had been before now. She would have remembered having this Demon in the building before. She sipped her water and realised how rude she was being. She wasn't normally so uncouth as to stare. She turned away, finished her much needed water and disposed of the paper cup into the rubbish bin that sat beside the water cooler.

Her boss sat waiting for when she returned to her office. Security had reported the incident with Marius. *Great, another lecture on how to handle unruly Demons and another incident report to be filled out. Yet another fabulous day in the office. Not.*

She folded herself into the chair behind the desk and nodded in, hopefully the right places, as her boss ranted. Her mind was much more interested in her encounter with the gorgeous Demon in the waiting room. She needed to find out who he was and how their paths could cross again.

***

The rest of the week, following the encounter with the Demon stranger was much the same as she had every other week; clock watching, dealing with Demonic clients, trying to help them find work. The week had dragged on for what seemed like forever. But, when her mind wandered, there was one person – no one *Demon* – who filled it. She was glad it was Friday and she had the weekend to herself.

There was a standing rule in the building, under no circumstances were staff allowed to fraternise with the clientele. It didn't mean she had to stop her wicked mind coming up with scandalous situations with the mystery Demon.

She was deep in thought when Sally, one of her office colleagues and friends, sashayed into her office. A blindfold hung off the tips of her outstretched fingers.

"We have a surprise for you Evie." She smirked.

Eve groaned, she had a sneaking suspicion her co-workers would pull something like this. This was why she preferred to forget her birthday.

"Blindfold?"

"I can't just have you seeing what we have planned and spoiling the surprise." Sally positioned the blindfold over her eyes, plunging her into darkness.

She was led from her office and through the building. As they appeared to have reached their destination, she heard voices being hushed.

Sally untied the blindfold and as soon as it fell from her eyes, she peeled them open. The entire staff were assembled in the staff room and hollered, "*surprise!*" "Shouts of Happy Birthday followed."

On the table there was a small spread of finger food and a large black forest cake with a candle burning brightly in the middle. Her co-workers stood around smiling at her. She knew she was well liked around the office. She didn't hesitate to help other staff with either a problem or by covering their shifts if an emergency arose.

"Wow. Thank you." She was humbled by the effort they had gone to for her special day.

Sally handed Eve a paper plate and urged her to help herself from the fare on the table. They stood around eating, laughing and chatting until it came time for her cake.

Happy Birthday was sung and she blew out the candle. The scrumptious cake was then served. Eve glanced into the waiting room where there where several Demons waited to be seen by their case manager. Their faces registered curiosity with the proceedings.

Before her boss could close the door, shutting them away from prying eyes, their eyes locked. *Her* Demon, the object of so many of her fantasies, was here.

"After-work drinks tonight." Sally shovelled a forkful of cake into her mouth. "No excuses, it's your birthday and we are going to celebrate." Her statement was accented by the pointing of her plastic fork at Eve's chest.

Eve smiled. She wasn't a party girl. She rarely went out with her co-workers, although she was frequently invited to the Friday night drinks. She relented and agreed. "Ok, I'll come tonight. But, the first round is on you.

"Absolutely." Sally finished her slice of cake and went in search of something else to nibble on.

Chapter Two.

The lunch-break party wound down and, after thanking everyone, Eve headed back to her office. She picked up the top file from reception and noted her next client was a new one to her. He was being transferred to her because one of the new girls had left the job in tears.

She stepped into her office to find her new client had invited himself in and taken a seat. What was it about Demons that they couldn't knock and wait to be invited in?

She noted, his black wings had a slight crimson sheen to them. *He's a Battle Demon.* Eve rounded her desk and sat down. She lay the file in front of her, opened it and perused the paperwork inside.

She alerted herself, Marius was a Battle Demon – the main reason for his volatility. She would need to be cautious with this one. The majority of demons she dealt with were of the Battle kind. Angry, volatile, unpredictable. Others such as Incubi, and the less prevalent Succubae, resisted coming into contact with humans. The exception were their 'feeders' – humans who were so enraptured with their Incubi and Succubae masters they didn't know or care that they were essentially pleasure slaves.

"Good afternoon, Mr. Decimus." Eve felt her pulse race as she gazed into his face. It was *him. Her* Demon. He was every bit as delicious as when she had first encountered him. His muscled body was to die for, and here he was, sitting across from her in her office. Her heart thumped against her ribs, her mouth dried.

"Good afternoon, and please, call me Decimus." His gorgeous smile lit up his face and caused her core to flood with excitement.

Oh god, his voice is even sexier than I remember. Eve shifted in her seat and gathered her composure. "Any luck finding work?" Eve's mind wandered to a few jobs around her house he could do her for… for her, she corrected. *Get your mind out of the gutter.*

She tilted her head and floated on his dreamy voice as he listed several places he had been to, trying to find work. So far, he had received no calls back. He had a clean police record, but was considered homeless and not to be trusted. He, along with other displaced Demons, lived in one of the decimated buildings in a slum area known as Demonville.

***

From the corner of her eye, Eve noted Decimus' eyes drink in her face and upper body as she wrote down what he had told her. A seductive smile never leaving his lips. She finished her interview with him and stood as he rose to leave. When he turned his back to her, her eyes zeroed in on his finely sculpted ass clad in blue jeans. She sighed as he strode from her office, negotiating the door with his broad shoulders and wingspan.

"Fuck that rule." Her breathing was raspy, she was in lust. She fought to compose herself and return to being the cool, calm and collected rehabilitation officer she was expected to be.

The next few working hours passed by in a blur. Clients came in, talked and left with minimal fuss. Her mind was far from being on her job. It had joined her body in being fixed on a certain Demon.

***

Sally collected her after they had finished their filing for the day, it was a welcome distraction. "Ready to go and get drunk?" Arm in arm they left the office and meeting up with a few of their co-workers at a bar.

The night was filled with laughter and plenty of alcohol. Their singing worsened as the night wore on and the alcohol flowed through their veins.

Eve, who rarely made a show of herself by dancing in public, and some of the girls got up and danced to the old juke box. When the song, *Evie*, started playing and her so-called friends began drunkenly screaming - *Evie let your hair hang down*, she shrivelled with embarrassment. The fact she was the object of amusement for other patrons of the bar, added to her discomfort.

When she could no longer take being the focus of everyone's attention, she insisted on returning to their booth. Their alcohol supplies had dwindled to a point her friends stated was simply not acceptable for a celebration of her birthday. Eve volunteered to go to the bar for the next round, she needed a breather.

As she stood attempting to snag the attention of the barman, a familiar but slurred voice breathed heavily into her ear.

"Hey baby, have you missed me?" His voice brought back unwelcome memories - finding him in bed with another woman, in *her* bed, in *her* house. His hand reached around her middle, thumb running against the underside of her breasts.

"Fuck off Jacob." Her alcohol fuzzy head cleared instantly as she pushed his hand away.

"Come on, baby, you know you miss me. Can't I give you a birthday present?" He manhandled her closer.

Eve fought to pull away. His hard-on brushed her leg through his jeans.

"Let me guess, your *present* is poking me in the ass right now." Eve hissed her disgust.

"Oh, baby. I know you'd just love to feel me inside you again." He ground himself against Eve.

Her anger burst forth as nausea bubbled in her throat. "I. Said. Fuck. Off. Jacob."

He sneered at her while raking is eyes over her body. "Nuh, uh, not until I have you again, babe. I remember what a great screw you were. I know you'd like me to drag you into the alley and fuck you until you can't see straight. It'd be like a tomcat and his slut."

Eve used every bit of strength she possessed and pushed at his chest. She felt unclean and uncomfortable being touched by such a sleaze. Jacob's arms tightened around her as she struggled. Eve started to panic and looked desperately over to the table where her friends were. They were deep in conversation and laughter, unable to see what was happening to their friend. The bar had gotten busier and louder, it was no use screaming out. Jacob dragged her away from the bar. Jacob's hands held her tight. Her resistance was useless.

It was a Demon who came to her rescue.

Her Demon.

Eve glanced through her tears at the wall of muscle, and the span of his wings as he fronted her captor. Relief flooded through her.

"I believe the lady told you to fuck off." His angry and deep rumbling voice caused shivers to dance down Eve's spine.

Jacob refused to release her and straightened to his full height – a full foot and a half shorter than the Demon. If the situation hadn't been so tense, Eve would have laughed at her ex's pathetic display of power. Or, was it weakness? "Back off Demon. Eve belongs to me. You're not wanted or needed. It's because of your kind, our earth has gone to shit."

Eve squeaked in pain as Jacob squeezed her tighter.

Decimus stiffened at Eve's cry of pain and distress. He glared down at the pathetic lowlife before him. He sucked in a deep breath, reached out and forcibly twisted the pathetic man's arms from her. He pulled Eve against his chest, her head tilted back and she smiled.

"Get the fuck out of here and if I see you around Miss Eve again, you won't get off so lightly." The Demon propelled Jacob toward the front door and he crashed through them.

Eve pushed herself free. "Thank you, Decimus."

"My pleasure, Miss Eve. Go back to your friends."

Eve moved away quickly, disappointed he seemed to want to be rid of her. She slipped through the growing crowd to the bar to order drinks.

She sat on a stool, placed her order and peered over the bar in search of her rescuer. He was sitting in a corner with three other Demons. Three human women were sitting either on or beside them, they were running their hands over the Demons muscular bodies and literally drooling.

Eve knew there were incubi amongst the ranks of the Demons and wondered if any were among Decimus' friends. The Demons were complex in their hierarchy, comprising Battle Demons as well as those who incited the seven deadly sins. Pride, Gluttony, Sloth, Wrath, Lust, Greed and Envy were planted into the hearts of weak men and women. Her studies, and conversations with her clients, had enlightened Eve about the Demon structure. Inciters of the seven deadly sins were scattered across the world and almost all were male. Although vast, the incubi and succubi numbers did not compare with those of the Battle Demons who had been abandoned on earth.

Nobody could doubt, Decimus was a Battle Demon. His imposing frame and domineering presence screamed, *run for your life, or you'll get your ass handed to you by this motherfucker.*

Decimus' gaze fixed on her. Her mouth dried and her body trembled. Her core flooded with the need for sexual release. It was commonly known, all Demons harbored a part of the *Seven* within them. There was no question she lusted after Decimus. Had he planted it within her with his brief touch?

She slid from the stool and collected the tray filled with their drinks. She threaded her way back to the booth and her friends. After placing the tray on the table, she slid into the booth.

Sally leaned over and shouted over the din. "What took you so long?"

"Had a run-in with my ex."

"Oh, the one who you caught…"

"Yes." Eve cut her off.

"That must have been awkward." Sally lifted her *Sex on the Beach* cocktail and sipped.

"I had help to get away from him." Eve glanced to where Decimus sat. A drunken, busty blonde was licking the side of his face in an attempt to entice him to kiss her.

Eve stiffened at the sight. Was she jealous?

Decimus pushed the blonde off onto one of his Demon friends and crossed his arms over his muscular chest. The blonde slut lowered her head into her new conquest's lap. Eve watched as the blonde's head bobbed up and down. There was no confusion as to what was taking place.

Sally followed the line of Eve's gaze. "Ugh, some women have no self-respect." She tipped the glass back and swallowed the last of her cocktail.

Eve pried her eyes from her rescuer and tried to enjoy the rest of the evening.

Chapter Three.

By the time Eve was ready to leave the bar and her birthday celebration behind, her vision was a touch blurry and she was extremely unsteady. The bouncers had begun moving people out and the lights dipped, indicating last call for drinks.

Sally had hooked up with Frank from the office. *Again.* They were nowhere to be seen. Eve had lost count of how many times these two had hooked up. It was always when her friend was drunk and she knew, come morning, Sally would be overwhelmed with regret that she had again fallen victim to Frank's charms.

Eve struggled to her feet and bid the rest of her co-workers, goodnight. *Happy Birthdays* rang out as she stumbled toward the door in a drunken haze.

The cool night air was refreshing but did little to clear the fuzziness from her head. She stumbled along the street, not realising she was being followed. She was too shocked to scream out when someone from behind pushed her into an alley.

She spun around to be confronted once more by her ex. "Jacob. What the fuck?" Eve pushed at him violently.

"I thought we'd pick up where we left off before that fucker Demon interrupted us, baby." He pushed her hard against a brick wall. She was held firm with his arm pinned across her chest. Footsteps sounded in the alleyway heralding possible rescue. Hope rippled through her.

Jacob glanced to his side. "Oh yeah, meant to mention, some of my friends want to join in the fun. But, I get first taste."

Eve fought like a wildcat as he pulled her skirt up, shoved his hand inside her panties and fondled her pussy.

Hope of rescue fled when Jacob's friends edged ever closer.

His fingers scratched at her folds, she screamed herself hoarse to no avail. "It's been a while babe, hope you remember I like it rough." She noted his leer in the dim light of the alley.

Eve spat at him, which earned her a hard slap across the face. Her cheek throbbed and blood trickled into her mouth from her lip.

Jacob pushed her roughly to the ground. She felt skin tear from her elbows and knees. Tears filled her eyes. He stood over her.

"Ungrateful slut, I'll teach you some damned respect." He dragged her up by her hair. Her head reeled back as he slapped her face again. "You want to act like a bitch? Then I'll take you like one." He reefed her skirt over her ass.

"How about I teach *YOU* some respect, asshole." A thunderous voice echoed through the alleyway.

Jacob spun around. "Who the fuck? You. I'll teach you to interrupt my fun, Motherfucker. Get him boys, but leave some for me. This is the second time tonight he's interfered with my fun."

Eve watched as a winged avenger strode toward them.

Jacob fisted Eve's hair, holding her firm while his two friends moved to attack Decimus. The Demon moved swiftly, intercepting the moving fist of the first of his attackers. He crushed the hand in his vice-like grip, the man squealed in pain. Decimus twisted the shattered bones as the man collapsed to the ground. The other leapt on Decimus' back, attempting to slam his fist into the back of the Demon's head.

With a sharp snap of his wings, Decimus threw the man from his back. He skidded across the concrete of the alley coming to a stop amongst scattered rubbish bins.

Jacob released Eve with a promise to be back for her once all this was done with. He drew a switchblade from his pocket and flicked the business end out to gleam menacingly in the dim light of the alley.

He rushed Decimus. "Come on you Demon fuck, think you can play with another man's bitch?" His body was primed for attack. Decimus stood patiently, his hands clasped in front of him.

He spoke quietly, his voice menacing. "You have threatened Miss Eve twice tonight. Now you have injured her. You will now pay."

Decimus propelled himself toward Jacob, mowing him down. They grunted and rolled as they fought beside Eve. She scooted back against the brick wall of the alley. She couldn't see most of what was going on as Decimus' wings blocked her view of the fight. Grunts of pain filled the air.

Decimus rose and swung toward her. His wings were outstretched, Jacob's throat tightly gripped in his hand. He lifted the hapless fool and held him above his head.

"Touch her again, and I will kill you." With a flick of his wrist he threw Jacob through the air. He crashed into a brick wall and slid to the ground. Unconscious.

With his job done, he turned to Eve. She cowered against the brickwork and he hurried toward her. The air moved around her as he approached, his wings acted as fans. The fetid smells of piss and booze from the alley wafted up to her nose. There was the smell of something else too. Something familiar, blood.

Decimus crouched before her. "Are you alright?" His hand rested lightly on her arm.

Eve peered up at him through the tears in her eyes. She nodded before launching herself into his arms. She felt safe, warm as his arms wrapped comfortingly around her.

She inhaled his scent as she whispered against his neck. "Thank-you." His odour was spicy, masculine. A throbbing need shot through her body. She wanted to be with him, under him, and have him deep inside her. She was shocked with the depth of her feelings for a man she had known for such a short time.

Decimus helped her up, setting her onto her feet. She noticed his wince.

"Are you ok?" She placed her hand on his abdomen to steady herself. It came away wet with blood.

"Shit" Eve glanced at her bloodied hand and back to his face. "Decimus, you've been stabbed. We have to get you to a hospital."

Decimus looked down. "Hospital?" He pressed a hand to the cut in his tank top, blood seeped out over his fingers. "That's not necessary."

"I beg to differ with you. You're bleeding profusely and there's no telling what damage he's done to your internal organs." Adrenalin, triggered by the sight of his injury, jolted her to awareness. Her drunken fog cleared. She glanced at his hand pressed over the wound. "Keep your hand there, and apply pressure, it should help to stem the bleeding." When she looked back up, pain lines marred his handsome face.

"Come with me, there's a hospital not too far from here. She tugged on his hand. Bewildered and in pain, he followed her. His hand remained firmly pressed against his wound as they moved through the darkened streets of the city. They passed by buildings still under repair toward the brightly lit hospital. Their temporary scaffolding and security fencing giving the city a run-down appearance.

They checked Decimus in at the Emergency Department, and were handed a number. Eve felt unsettled.

The last time she had been here had been a year ago. It was the last time she had seen her brother alive, and he had been barely that. She felt small sitting beside Decimus' powerful figure. She was worried with how he hunched forward, his face taut with pain. People glared at them, mouths stretched in a thin line of disgust. How dare a Demon enter their hospital.

Hours passed as they waited among the sickly and injured in the over-crowded waiting room. Now and again, an ambulance arrived with some poor unfortunate being rushed to the care of the emergency doctors on staff.

"Number seventy-three please." The voice of the nurse sounded stressed, under pressure.

Decimus rose stiffly to his feet, the wound poured with blood. Eve took his hand and assisted him through the open door, past the nurse. His touch was cool.

"You're warm." He smiled at her weakly.

The nurse showed them to a cubicle where a bed rested against the wall. She eyed Decimus warily. "Please remove your shirt and sit on the bed so I can assess your wound."

He attempted to comply with the request but Eve watched as he struggled. She worried about his weakness and moved to help him divest himself of his torn tank.

Eve's eyes raked his body. She licked her lips. Oh how she would love to climb over that mountain of muscle and stake a claim on those lips. She felt her face heat at the thought.

The nurse worked to clean up the wound to clearly assess it.

Eve felt the nurse, although dutiful, was trying to rid herself of them as quickly as possible. She stitched him up and wrapped a bandage around his middle. After handing Eve a small dose of pain killers for her Demon, she gave them instructions to keep the wound clean and a date to return to have stitches removed. She escorted them out and called for the next patient.

Decimus nodded and thanked the nurse who graced them with a small smile. Eve checked Decimus out and paid for the medical services before joining him at the hospital's exit.

She threaded her arm through his. "Do you have a place to stay?"

Images of his 'home' sprang to mind. A small, filthy, recovered mattress was his bed on the hard concrete floor. He didn't have much in the way of clothing or possessions.

"I have a small place in Demonville."

Eve frowned. She'd heard about the squalid, filthy conditions. "Demonville is not a place you should be while you are injured. My place is close by, you can stay until you're healed."

The clouds above chose that moment to dump their contents on them in the form of blinding rain. They hurried to the train station as fast as Decimus' injury would allow.

Eve gripped his hand tightly.

"If it's no trouble for you."

They headed down to the subway. Most of the lines had been repaired allowing trains to run in the inner city and northern suburbs.

Eve deposited two tokens into the slot at the turnstiles and they descended the steps to the platform. She glanced around. Three cavorting drunken teens and a bedraggled man were the only other people waiting for the next train. The bedraggled man took comfort in his brown paper bag, no doubt it concealed a bottle of cheap booze. He muttered nonsense to himself between swigs.

Decimus moved closer to Eve, a gesture of protection. She watched as his eyes assessed each person's threat to the woman he stood beside.

"How's the pain?" Eve noted the strain on his face.

"I'm trying to ignore it but it throbs and feels hot, painful. Where I'm from, pain is something you get used to and we use it to our advantage. People on your world are weakened by it. People on my world use pain to grow and become someone stronger. We push through the torment, we don't allow it to drag us down."

He looked down at Eve as the train pulled in and screeched to a stop, metal against metal. The doors hissed open, Eve assisted Decimus inside before sitting on the torn and stained bench seat. He stood protectively over her, his eyes searching for any potential threat to his female.

His female? He helps her out, and suddenly he thinks of this little female as *his?* From the moment he had witnessed her shaking at the water cooler following her encounter with Marius, he had been enthralled with her. He had been with human women before, the hussies practically threw themselves at him and other Demons when they frequented the bar. Demons loved sex. The pure sinfulness of the act spoke to them on a spiritual level. Decimus was not one to forgo the carnal pleasures that were offered him by the Demon's fan girls.

Eve though, was different. His body responded to her closeness like never before.

Eve studied Decimus, watching for signs of discomfort or pain. He smiled reassuringly at her as they rode the train in silence.

They alighted the train at the seventh stop, Eve led the way while tightly gripping his hand. They moved across the platform and away from the crowd before Eve spoke. "How are you feeling?"

Decimus grunted. "It feels felt like Lucifer spat his noxious spittle, added salt crystals and pissed into the wound. Other than that, I'm fine."

Eve glanced at him. "Quite a descriptive way of admitting you have pain. Won't be long and you can rest." She led him down a quiet street with well-kept houses. The kind you might have wanted to buy before the war made the world just a bit harder to bear. She opened the squeaky gate of a single storey weatherboard house and fumbled for in her purse for her keys.

She stepped back after unlocking her door and allowed Decimus to enter first. Eve watched as he sidled into her home. His big frame jostling its way through the door caused a few feathers to come loose from his wings. Her eyes followed them as they floated to the ground.

Eve glanced back up in time to see the curtains across Mrs. Hobbs' front window in the house across the road, fall back into place.

***

Edwina Hobbs was the local busybody. She was an obsessive Christian so needless to say, her opinion of Demons wallowed down in the gutter. She was never seen without her pocket bible reclined in her hands.

When Eve had first been employed counselling Demons, Mrs Hobbs and a few of her cronies had cornered her. They had preached righteously to her about denying Demons any kind of help. They ranted about how Demons were the spawn of the Devil, and God would cast judgement on her for helping them. Her only salvation would be to repent and quit her job.

Leaving her job was not about to happen any time soon and it certainly wouldn't be because her neighbors demanded it. Her response had been simple. She had folded her arms over her chest in defiance and stated, "When God gets back, please be sure to let me know. I'll invite him and the Devil over for tea and biscuits. We can all discuss where my mortal soul should go. But, until then I have bills to be paid and I do have a need to eat every day." The women had been mortified.

"I assume you won't feed me and pay my bills, will you?" She resisted the urge to laugh at the look of horror on Mrs. Hobbs' face "No? Shame. I'll just have to continue to work with the Devil's minions then. Have a lovely day and please don't forget to give God my address." The group of do-gooders had spun on their heels and huffed off.

***

Decimus stood in the entry of her two-bedroom house and scanned the small rooms. Eve loved her home and it carried both happy and sad memories. She had shared the place with her brother, Sam. Pictures of the two of them adorned the walls. A small display case was filled with trophies and pictures of older model cars. Cars which had been overhauled for showing and burnout competitions. Her favorite picture was one of Sam smiling. He had removed his helmet and had his arms wrapped around two busty blonde *grid girls*.

Decimus wondered who the man in the pictures was and why he caused Eve's eyes to fill with sadness when she looked at his face.

"Come through, you can have my brother's bed. I'll check on your dressing and stitches in the morning." She led the Decimus down the hallway to the back of the house. "The bathroom is right across from your room." She switched on the light in Sam's room, before turning and colliding against the warmth of his chest. He steadied her with his large, calloused hands and peered down at her.

"Thank you for helping and taking care of me." His voice rumbled in his chest as he spoke sending flashes of warmth and desire through her body.

Eve despaired at the loss when Decimus released her. She'd enjoyed being in his arms. "No, thank you for rescuing me. I'm sorry you were hurt in the process. Consider staying here, repayment for helping me."

Decimus smirked as he turned his back to her and entered the room. *I can think of several other ways you could repay me which would be far more interesting.* His thoughts wandered to images of her naked beneath him. His strong hands caressing her luscious breasts, teasing the nipples to hard, rosy buds. His tongue lapping at the curve of her neck where her shoulder joined. Savouring every inch of her, slowly, methodically.

Her voice broke into his thoughts but he hadn't heard what she had said. When glanced over his shoulder, she was gone. The effects of his erotic thoughts, hadn't. His cock strained for release from his jeans.

Decimus sighed and struggled to free himself from the blue linen top the hospital had given him in place of his tank. Eventually he peeled off his clothes, layer by layer. After folding them neatly, he placed them on a chair in the corner.

He was stark naked as he approached the bed. He heard Eve's loud gasp and spun around, ready to defend her. He froze, bent forward, primed for attack.

Eve stood riveted to the spot by the doorway. She clutched a bright pink towel to her chest, her face was several shades brighter. "Oh my. I'm..., uh..., I brought you this…." Her voice faded as he straightened before her. His body was male perfection. Abs hard and sculpted, pectorals - magnificent. His waist was narrow and his 'v' muscles led down to a long, thick and deliciously hard cock. His jet-black wings arched upward framing his body with glorious darkness. "A… a towel for the morning so you can shower. She extended her arm and held the towel toward him.

Decimus smiled and stepped forward. Eve swallowed nervously. Her eyes seemingly developed a mind of their own and insisted on capturing every inch of his perfect manhood. She chastised herself and raised her eyes to his face. His eyes were filled with knowing desire as he accepted the towel. Their fingers brushed and jolts of electricity zapped through her. She trembled and stepped back.

"I'll... My room is two doors down if you need anything. Good-night."

She fled from the bedroom, his body burned into her mind.

Decimus leaned forward and poked his head through the doorway. He followed the sway of her hips as she moved. His eyes drank in every curve of Eve's delicious figure. He watched until she vanished into her room. The door closed with a loud bang.

He sighed and returned to the bed slipping under the covers. It was comfortable, the faint scent of another male drifted from the pillow and mattress. He inhaled, sniffing the air. This room hadn't been used by a male in almost a year. Decimus shifted to position his wings and his wounded side to where they were most comfortable and fell into sleep.

Chapter Four.

Soft humming floated into the room as Decimus awoke. Sunlight flooded the room. Taps squeaked and the sound of water reached his ears. Eve was showering. He knew he shouldn't but he couldn't resist the urge to move so he could see from his room to the bathroom. The door was open! His cock flinched as his eyes locked on a very nice view of her naked bottom before she stepped into the shower.

Decimus continued to watch until the glass of the shower steamed up and cut off his view. Eve's body was perfect. As she moved, his hand found its way to his engorged and now throbbing cock. Up and down, his hand moved faster as she caressed her body with her lathered hands. He could almost feel his own hands tracing every inch of her perfection. His cock grew thicker, harder, almost painfully so.

When she lifted her hands to her hair to lather the shampoo, he groaned. Her already perky breasts stood even more upright. He thumb grazed the tip of his cock, his free hand cupped his balls. His head lolled back onto the pillows as he reached a thundering climax. His cock erupted like a volcano spewing ribbons of cum onto his belly and blood stained sheets.

He felt like he'd returned to his beloved Hell. Never had he experienced such a violent and fiery orgasm. What was it about this woman that forced him to lose his control?

Decimus allowed himself a few moments to recover and rose from the bed. His body felt damp. When he inspected his side, the bandages were soaked with fresh blood. He carefully removed it. The stitches had burst during the night and his wound now lay open. It showed no signs of healing and Decimus frowned. Demons normally healed much faster than humans, why did it still appear so raw?

Forgoing his clothes so as not to cover them with blood, he slipped across the hall and knocked on the now closed bathroom door.

Eve opened the door with a blinding smile that shot warmth straight to his heart. Her hair was wrapped up in a towel and she was dressed in a bright purple bath robe.

"Morning." It took a moment for her to notice his nakedness and the further south her eyes wandered, the more heated she felt. When she caught sight of the bleeding, she paled. "Shit, your stitches have torn." She dragged him into the bathroom, his nakedness forgotten for the moment. "I have medical strips that should hold the wound closed."

Decimus allowed her to guide him to sit on the closed lid of the toilet. She dropped to her knees to closer inspect the damage. The wound was clean and showed signs of healing around the edges. "I think you'll live but we need to stop the bleeding." She rose to her feet and filled the basin before rummaging in a wall cabinet and adding a few drops of medical disinfectant to the warm water. She lifted out a bag of cotton balls. With soft and gentle strokes, she cleaned the blood from around his wound, patting it dry with a clean washcloth.

Decimus' breath grew erratic. She felt him tremble beneath her touch. His eyes shone with lust.

Her own hand trembled as she brushed his muscular chest. She placed adhesive strips across the open wound, bringing the two raw edges of flesh together.

The heat of desire was palpable and she lay her small hand against his chest.

Decimus growled, the sound rising from deep in his throat. He reached over and pulled the towel from her head. Her damp locks tumbled over her shoulders. His fingers wove within them before he cupped her face in his hands and tilted her head upward.

"You are a beautiful, caring woman, Eve. You deserve to be worshipped and loved for the rest of your life." His head lowered and he grazed his lips against hers. Would she reject him? Leave him to find his own way in this world, alone.

His cock jolted with anticipated pleasure surprised when she wrapped her arms around his neck and deepened their kiss. Her fingertips brushed the join between feather and skin causing his feelings to cascade out of control. It was the most sensitive part of his body, aside from his dick, and the pleasure she was giving him was extraordinary. His tongue forced its way into her mouth, demanding, wanting.

When they broke away, they were breathless. "I am led to believe, Demons are masters of sex and are consummate lovers." Eve's voice was thick with need.

"We do like to fuck, long and hard. We engage many positions, techniques and styles to bring our partners many satisfying completions. We are also much better endowed than human males." Decimus grinned at her cheekily. "Would you care to sample my wares?"

His muscular arms wound around her warm body, pulling her closer. His tongue caressed her lips, demanding entry. She obliged, her lips parted and she moaned softly as he again explored her mouth. His hands roamed over her body. He pulled at the sash of her robe opening her body to him. He pushed it from her shoulders, it whispered to the floor.

He laved at her neck, her jaw. She tasted like nothing he had ever experienced before.

Eve's desire rose and she sucked and kissed at his face, his jaw, his neck. He was sweet, masculine with a touch of spice. And, all male. Exceptional male.

He drew away from her, his black eyes flamed red with want. Her heart jackhammered against her ribs as she waited for him to resume devouring her. Inch by glorious inch. She wanted him like she had wanted no other.

He lifted her into his arms and deposited her bare ass onto the cold of benchtop. She squealed as the cold jolted her.

Decimus stood back holding her hands away from her body as he perused what was before him. Perfect breasts, creamy flesh topped with deep rosy nipples hardened to nubs. They were like a decadent desert topped with a delicious cherry. A dessert that would tantalize his taste buds.

He licked his lips and Eve watched his eyes darken to stormy gray. His mouth dived onto her nipple, sucking, nipping. His other hand, not wanting her other nipple to feel left out, tweaked and pinched.

Eve moaned and pushed her breast further into his mouth. She couldn't seem to get enough of this incredible man. Her back arched, her fingers dragged through his thick dark hair. She needed him closer. Her arousal was complete, juices flooded her core and dripped onto her thighs.

Decimus' hands were like magic as they left the job of worshipping her breasts to his mouth and sought out every inch of her body. His fingers were everywhere. Everywhere he brushed erupted with desire. She wriggled and squirmed under his touch.

Decimus glanced up at her as widened her thighs. His fingers caressed her curls before slipping inside her folds. Her back arched as he thumbed her already swollen clit.

Eve caressed the tips of his black wings and he moaned with delight. They were so sensitive to her touch. Lust, like he had never felt before, overwhelmed him. His wings trembled making a soft rustling sound. His mouth released her nipple with a soft pop and lowered between her legs.

His tongue joined the fingers inside her folds. He stretched her wide. He nipped at her clit while his fingers delved ever deeper. Her head lolled back, she was floating with ecstasy.

Her gasping moans turned into cries of deep bliss. She writhed on the bench top pleading for more.

Decimus' hands clamped down on her thighs, holding her firmly in place. The feeling of being held fast by this strong, seductive Demon thrilled her and she playfully fought against him. His response was to hold her even tighter as he savoured her taste. He pulled away and licked her nectar from his lips before he rose.

"I want you." His voice was husky with need.

Eve was desperate for him. "Then take me." Her arms wrapped around his neck, she pulled him closer.

His lips crashed against hers, he teased her entrance with his engorged cock. She moaned into his mouth and eased herself nearer his cock. He pushed through her wet folds until he was deep inside. His thrusts were slow at first, gentle. As their need for each other grew, they clutched at each other. Their fucking was frenzied.

Her hands caressed his wings, he groaned with delight. They folded to surround her, fluttering with excitement. It was obvious his wings were sensitive to her touch.

Eve's legs wrapped around his thrusting hips, her nails raked the flesh of his back and her ass slipped back and forth on the bench.

Decimus snaked his hand between them, his fingers settled over her swollen clit and stroked gently, persistently.

Eve arched her back, her vision dimmed as she was pushed closer and closer to the edge. That incredible, soul liberating edge. She crashed over amid screams, Decimus' name on her lips.

Decimus tensed as his own climax neared. A few more thrusts, he threw back his head and growled her name. It was beastly, unearthly but passionate. Ribbons of cum flowed from the tip of his cock into her eager passage.

They had hit paradise together, wrapped in each other's arms. Eve lowered her head to his chest and listened as his heart beat erratically. She smiled as she floated down from the high of her orgasm. She had affected this mountainous Demon as much as he had affected her. orgasm.

His hands wandered her back in a soothing motion as they completed their descent together.

"Are you all right?" Decimus' voice remained thick with desire.

"Hmmm." Eve was lost in an orgasmic stupor.

"I'll take that as a yes." Decimus leaned forward to kiss her.

Eve gently pulled herself away and slid from the bench onto wobbly legs. Decimus caught her and held her close.

"I feel like a new-born foal. I have never been so weak after sex before."

"You, my love, have been fucked by a Demon. We love the way we live – hard and fast." His fingers curled beneath her chin and he tilted her head. His lips capturing hers caused them both to tremble with want.

Warmth radiated from his wings. When their lips parted, she lowered her head and took first one nipple, then the other, into her mouth. He groaned, his wings trembled. Reluctantly she pulled away. This, whatever it was, couldn't continue. She was human, he was a Demon. Natural enemies.

Fuck, I'll take all I can this weekend and make memories for when it is over.

"Decimus, I know I'm being forward and I would never usually ask. Hell, I would never normally have sex with someone I've only just met. Would you like to stay with me for the weekend?"

"I don't know. I have nothing planned except for maybe a few drinks with friends. Are you sure? I'd hate to get you into trouble at your job. I know there are strict rules about us fraternizing."

"I won't tell if you don't. If you find that seeing me as a professional in the office is uncomfortable, then we can get another rehab officer to take over your file. Unless of course, you don't *want* to stay with me." She sucked her bottom lip between her teeth, a habit she had when she was nervous.

Decimus leaned forward and captured her lips. He drew her lip from between her teeth into his mouth. She moaned softly, deepening the kiss as she leaned into him.

He pulled away. "Does that feel like the kiss of a Demon who doesn't want to stay? As for the office, I don't want another counsellor. It might be advisable for you to get something more private though. I may find it hard to keep my hands to myself after this weekend."

Eve felt his hard cock rub against her belly. Her nipples stiffened but her stomach chose that exact moment of passion to growl. Her face heated with embarrassment. "Hungry?" She trailed her fingers over his chest.

"For you. I could eat you all day long and still not be satisfied." He brushed his lips against her ear.

Eve pushed away. "If you want more of me, I have to eat. I need my strength to keep up with you." She squealed as he leaned forward and his teeth nipped her soft lobe.

He held her tight, not wanting to let her go. He nipped and sucked her lips. She tried in vain to move him away. The man, more and more she thought of him as a man not a Demon, was built like an immovable wall. She squirmed and protested. "I need to eat, why don't you have a shower while I prepare us something?"

He loosened his hold and she took the opportunity to duck under his wing. Her fingers caressed the edge as she made her escape and moved away. It fluttered with excitement and her eye caught the movement as Decimus' cock jumped and lengthened. *Hmmm, his wings and dick are certainly connected in some way.* She would file this information away. It could be very useful. She slipped down the hallway.

"Damn that woman." Decimus muttered as his hard on began throbbing.

Chapter Five

Decimus showered, the hot water felt luxurious on his tired body. He smiled as he dried off with the fluffy pink towel. *If only the other Demons could see me now.* He wrapped it around his girth and returned to the room where he had slept.

His eyes took in his unmade bed. The sheets were a bloodied and semen stained mess, he stripped them from the bed and dropped them onto the floor. His clothes hadn't fared much better. His jeans had a large streak of blood down one leg. The tank top he'd recovered as they'd left the hospital had a large hole and was covered in blood down one side. He didn't fancy wearing the hospital issued shirt again, he would dispose of it into the trash.

Leaving the towel in place and gathering the clothing and sheets, he walked out to the kitchen. "I bled on your brother's sheets. I hope he won't be too angry. My clothes are also spattered with blood."

Eve was bent over rummaging in her fridge. Her short summer dress revealed the thong she was wearing. His breath caught, his cock hardened and the towel tented.

Eve turned from the fridge, a carton of eggs and a packet of bacon in hand. "He won't be angry. Sam, died in a car accident about a year ago."

She placed the food on the bench and removed the laundry from his arms. He watched as she left the kitchen through a door next to the fridge. He sat on a stool at the breakfast bar and heard a series of beeps before she returned. He had noted the sadness in her eyes when she spoke of her brother.

"I'm sorry for your loss."

Eve shrugged. "Life happens, it's not always fair but it happens." She removed a bowl from an overhead cupboard cracked several eggs into it. She stood with her back to him. "I guess you have to work through the grief and deal with it." She grabbed a whisk from the drawer beside her. Her movements mesmerized him as she whisked the eggs into a golden froth.

Decimus stood and moved toward her when he noticed tears glistening in her eyes. His hands slipped up her sides, her dress slid up, exposing her thighs. He pressed himself against her back, feeling the warmth of her body through the dress. His lips sought out the juncture where her neck and shoulders met, nuzzling her long hair out of his way.

Eve tilted her head back into his kiss and sighed softly. Her unshed tears broke free and he spun her around. He held her and kissed away the tears as they fell. Never had she been treated with such tenderness. His hands cupped her ass as he nibbled her ear. Tears gave way to arousal.

Decimus' fingers fondled her body before slipping inside her lace panties. She was wet, ready for him. Her clit swollen. Moans filled the air as he suckled her neck.

Eve trembled under his fingertips. Decimus allowed the towel to slip from his hips, freeing his anxious cock. He pushed Eve's dress up to reveal the round globes of her ass. Sunlight spilled over her body as light flooded through the uncovered kitchen window.

As he ravaged her lips, his hand ripped the flimsy lace panties from her body. His talented fingers thrust inside her drenched folds. Her legs weakened. His engorged cock teased her, rubbing against her belly. It was not where she wanted him to be. She wanted, no needed, him inside her. Now!

"I need you," Eve gasped, She moved herself ever closer. She wanted to climb into his skin.

Decimus teased her until she could take no more. She turned in his arms and, after moving the bowl to where it would be safe, she bent forward over the bench. Her legs spread wide, inviting him into her wetness.

Decimus teased her folds with the head of his cock, coating it in her slick juices.

"Oh." Eve moaned as she lay her head against the cool surface of the bench. Decimus pushed her dress up over her head. He slipped the head of his cock into her entrance, his fingers still working her swollen nub. Her body trembled with pleasure as he worked her arousal. He spread her legs wider, she was pushed further against the bench as he bent her knees and lifted her feet from the floor. Her hands spread out on the bench helping to anchor her body.

Her Demon slammed inside her, she arched her back and he plundered her mercilessly.

His fingers caressed her back, flipped the catch on her bra, before moving up and fisting her hair. Tingles danced down her spine as he pulled her head backward and speared deep inside. His hands were everywhere, on her breasts, on her clit, her back, in her hair. Had he grown one or two extra?

Her cries echoed through her home as he relentlessly pounded her cunt. His lips nibbled and kissed. Wings encircled them both, fluttering excitedly as their climaxes rushed headlong to meet.

Decimus plunged over the edge and roared out his pleasure. His seed spewed forth, filling her. Eve was milliseconds behind him. She screamed out his name as she arched her back and pushed herself into him. She soared with the stars. Her orgasm so powerful it threatened to send her spiralling into darkness.

Their breathing was ragged as they descended together. Decimus lifted her into his arms and devoured her lips in a passionate kiss. They trembled in each other's arms, cocooned in the safety and protection of his wings.

"Sorry. I have never come before a woman but I couldn't hold back. I have never been with someone so fuckable." He smiled sheepishly.

Eve ran her tiny, sift hand down his face. "I'm glad I make you feel so good, cause you to lose control. You have no need to apologize." She reached for her dress.

Decimus placed his hand over hers. "Please, leave that off. You have no need for clothes today, or tomorrow. I want you naked. I want to worship your body."

Decimus' tone was almost demanding but Eve didn't mind. "What *will* the neighbours think?" She raised an eyebrow, her tone – teasing."

Decimus leaned in close, his eyes alight with sexual deviancy. "To Hell with them." He closed his eyes as he inhaled her scent.

Eve nipped playfully at the join between his neck and his wings. He closed his eyes and groaned. "If you keep doing things like that you are going to be very sore before the day is out. Not to mention starving."

Eve smiled at him. "I'll make breakfast if you can manage to keep your hands to yourself. Can you get me the apron hanging up behind the door?" Eve turned back to the half-beaten eggs.

Decimus put the apron on her, tying the strings around her back. He gave her ass a good sharp slap and smiled at the red hand print left behind.

Eve yelped. Her ass cheek flamed with heat. She glared at her Demon.

He laughed before propping himself against a cupboard nearby. He watched as she made scrambled eggs and bacon on toast.

Eve served their food and he followed her to the table.

Decimus ate with gusto, the pleasure on his face at the simple meal warming her heart.

"Decimus?"

"Yes." He didn't pause from shovelling the food into his mouth but raised his eyes.

"Is there a connection between your wings and your cock?"

His hand froze with his fork raised in mid-air. Food slipped back onto his plate. "Why do you ask?" This was a Demon's deepest secret. If their enemies knew their wings could be erotically aroused and affect their judgement, it would be used to weaken and conquer them.

"I noticed when we were fucking, if I lightly touched them with my fingers, they shivered and your cock got harder."

"You must tell no-one or it will be our downfall. When our wings are caressed they become aroused the same as our cocks. We feel as much pleasure through them as we do through our dicks."

"So I can cause you to become aroused just by fondling your wings?"

"Yes, but only when the edges are lightly caressed."

Eve smiled. "I won't mention this to anyone and I doubt your enemies would want to get close enough to fondle your wings. I think you, and others of your kind, are safe."

"Thank you." Decimus finished his meal and sat back with a satisfied look on his face.

Eve collected their dishes and padded to the sink.

Movement in the yard next door as she stood washing the dishes, caught her eye. Mrs. Hobbs was visiting Miss Wembley, another like-minded *Christian.* The scowls on the women's faces as Mrs. Wembley gestured to her house caused her temper to simmer. Eve had a bad feeling when it came to the two mean, conniving bitches.

Decimus strolled up behind her, leaned around and placed a kiss on her cheek. His arms and wings circled her.

Eve saw the moment her neighbours noticed the movement and the look of utter shock and revulsion on their faces was priceless. Eve smiled at the two bitches before flipping her middle finger up and lowering the blind.

***

The rest of the morning was spent cuddling on the couch. She had shown him some of her life, and opened her heart to him. She would not normally open herself up to someone she had known for such a short time. But, there was a first time for everything. After all, she had *never* had a weekend fling before.

She lay content in his arms, when Decimus whispered in her ear. She gazed up and nodded before they retreated to her bedroom.

She rifled through her closet, locating silken ties from her robes. She spun around holding them out. "Will these do?" Decimus grinned mischievously.

"On your knees, sweetheart." He indicated the floor before him.

"Yes, Sir." She moved quickly to kneel before him.

He paused. She looked so vulnerable kneeling before him. "You're sure you are okay with this? I promise I won't hurt you and if you are uncomfortable at any time, use the safety word we discussed."

"I want to try. Please?"

He accepted the silk ties from her. He secured one around her eyes, ensuring she wouldn't be able to see.

She trembled in anticipation as her Demon lover moved around her. With her lack of vision, her other senses came to full alert.

The other silk tie slid over her back, his hand pushed firmly against her, urging her forward. Eve placed her hands out to support herself as she dropped onto all fours. Decimus' hands caressed her back, moving slowly over the contours of her ass. She sucked in a deep breath.

She moaned softly, shuddering with sexual tension as he separated her ass cheeks and petted her moistening folds.

His tongue, warm and wet, sucked her shoulder causing her body to tingle. She encouraged his ministrations with soft moans and sighs of pleasure as he continued exploring her body.

Decimus paused to drink in the beautiful woman before him. His breath caught. He had one weekend and it was already half over. Eve was perfection. From the small scar on her chin to the chickenpox scar on her left butt cheek. Every part of his body prickled with desire. Never had he felt this way about anyone.

He knew he wanted to keep her, wanted to possess her, protect her from all the evil in the world. Yes, he would be classified as part of that evil but, he wasn't the Demon he had once been. His past days on Earth had seen him abandon the need for slaughter and cruelty. When his master had disappeared back to whichever Hell he had seen fit to return to, Decimus' desire for evil had gone with him.

He stroked his hard, aching cock as he worshipped the woman before him.

He lifted her into his arms and carried her to the side of the bed. After lowering her back to the floor, he sat down. "Lift your head sweetheart, open your mouth."

She did as he asked.

He reached over and drew her closer to him. Placing his hands on her head, he eased his cock into her sensuous mouth.

Eve took him willingly, her tongue flicked across the tip of his cock. He groaned and shuddered as she took him deep into her throat. Her teeth grazed the enlarged vein on the underside of his dick and his legs trembled, her soft, tiny hands cupped his balls. This woman would be his undoing. He couldn't think straight as she sucked him deep before pulling back until he almost slipped free.

He dragged at her hair when her tempo increased. How much more could he take? His cock was hard enough to drive nails. His muscles corded and tensed as his balls tightened. His climax came ever closer.

"Eve, I can't take any more. I need you sweetheart."

She shook her head and no matter how he tried to release himself, she held tight. Decimus knew he was beaten. He leaned back on his elbows, lifted his hips and thrust harder into her throat. When she groaned, the vibration against his cock threw him over the edge.

He shouted her name as ribbons of cum flooded her mouth. While he shuddered and shook, she milked every drop. Stars flashed before his eyes and yes, he hit the heights of heaven. When Eve continued to suckle him, his over sensitive cock begged for release. He was hardening again and it was sweet agony.

"Please, no more. Please, I need to be inside you."

Eve released his dick with a soft 'pop' and after licking cum from her lips, she smiled brightly.

"You have bewitched me woman. I have never been controlled by a person, like you control me."

He lifted her and placed her face down on the bed. After spreading her legs he tied first one ankle, and after removing the tie from her eyes, the other ankle to the bed posts. With her legs spread, her entrance was open for him to plunder. Decimus grabbed her hands placed them on the rungs of the bedhead.

"Don't move them."

A sharp slap stung her ass and she cried out. Her ass heated. "That's for disobeying me."

Another sharp slap, again she screamed and her cheek heated. Twice more he delivered ever hardening slaps to her ass. Tears formed in her eyes. It was a stinging pain verging on absolute pleasure.

Decimus leaned close to her ear. "Next time I ask you to release me, you will do so. I am your master, is that clear?"

"Yes, sir."

"Say it."

"You are my master." And, he was. .Eve felt inexplicably bound to her Demon. She was not ready to let him go. One weekend with this man would not be enough.

He dived onto her pussy, laving and licking her folds. Her ass rose into the air and she pushed closer to his mouth. He sucked her clit into his mouth and nibbled the swollen bud. She struggled to hang on to the rods but dared not disobey. When his fingers dove in alongside his tongue, she was done. She screamed his name over and over as wave after wave of climax bombarded her.

He plunged his painfully hard cock deep inside her as soon as she came down from the heights. His hands found her beaded nipples and twisted and pinched. Her moans intensified. Her core clenched around him, causing his cock to pulsate erratically. He arched his back and roared in satisfaction as his orgasm hit with such force, it blindsided him.

Eve was stretched to her limits as Decimus exploded inside her. Her orgasm crashed over her. She buried her face in the pillow and screamed at the top of her lungs. The man had thrown her into outer space and her eyes flashed.

A few moments later, they crashed back to earth.

Decimus shuddered before becoming still. He panted heavily and his sweat dripped onto her naked back. He pulled from, untied her ankles and rolled her onto her back.

"Are you all right?"

She smiled as she reached up and caressed his face. She rose slightly to press her lips against his. Her tongue sought his and his lips parted. Their kiss was sensuous, passionate.

"Shower?"

Decimus nodded. He swept her into his arms and padded to the shower.

Chapter Six

Eve and Decimus relaxed on the couch, entangled in each other's arms when a loud knock at the door startled them.

She removed his roaming hands from her breasts and tied her robe closed. "I wonder who it is at this time of night."

He raised his eyebrow. "Answering the door might give you a clue."

She smirked and padded to her front door. She cracked it open enough to see who was invading their peace. Mrs. Hobbs and four other women came into view. Eve opened the door further.

"Mrs. Hobbs. Is there an emergency? I wouldn't have expected you to be roaming the streets at this time of night, people might get the wrong idea." *Good one, go ahead and make things even worse. Provoke her even more than you already have by having a Demon in your home.*

The woman crossed her arms over her chest. All five glared at her, disgust radiating from them.

"Miss Macintyre. How dare you refer to me, and my colleagues, as street walkers. Especially when it has been brought to our attention, you are harbouring a *Demon* in your house."

"And, if I am? What business is it of yours?"

The woman glared at Eve. "Don't you realize you are in danger of being seduced by the Devil?"

"I hardly believe that, Mrs. Hobbs. You are aware, I work with Demons on a daily basis. I hardly believe having one as my guest will endanger me."

One of the entourage, Miss Wembley moved forward. "A guest? I don't think so. I *saw* you with him, giving yourself to him willingly. Have you no self-respect? Your body should only be given to your wedded husband, blessed by the good Lord himself. You have become a Demon's whore!"

It took all Eve's restraint not to burst into laughter at the woman's archaic outburst. "So, the local gossip is no longer feeding your curiosity, Miss Wembley. You have now become the area's *Peeping Tom*, what a sad and desperate life you must lead to stoop to such practices. Don't you think what one does in the privacy of one's home is just that – private?"

Miss Wembley wasn't to be shaken. "You have endangered all our lives by bringing that *thing* into our neighbourhood. I am protecting the good people of our area."

"By peeping through windows into your neighbour's homes? I wonder what they will think of your covert activities."

Mrs. Hobbs asserted her leadership and pushed Miss Wembley to the rear. "You must vanquish the evil creature and repent while your soul can still be saved." She waved a battered copy of the Holy Bible before her.

Eve felt the disturbance of air as her Demon slipped up beside her. His arm snaked around her waist and she was drawn against him. He pulled the door open as wide as it would go enabling the women to get a clear view.

The women gasped, and their faces were pinched with expressions of horror, at the sight of the naked Battle Demon standing beside the woman who harboured him.

His black wings hovered above them, shimmering. Light reflected off their crimson edges.

His voice was deep, decadent, like a delicious piece of warm chocolate. "Good evening, ladies, is there a problem here?"

Mrs. Hobbs recoiled and reached into her voluminous bosom. She pulled jewelled golden crucifix from their depths. "Beast, go back to Hell where you belong. You have no place here on Earth, seducing our young women." She waved the cross back and forth.

Decimus eyed the cross and smirked. "A nice piece of gold-plated tin, Mrs Hobbs. I'm not sure what you wish to achieve by waving it all over the place." He glanced at her cohorts. "Now ladies, if you'll excuse us, this beautiful woman and I have some hot, illicit and sinful activities to engage in." Decimus winked at the ladies before he swept Eve into his arms, spun around and kicked the door shut behind him.

She giggled into his shoulder. "I didn't have the greatest relationship with them before tonight, now I'd say it has gone to Hell in a handbasket."

"Does it bother you?" Decimus was concerned.

"Hell, no."

#

Eve luxuriated in bed, Decimus' possessive arms wrapped around her. One wing held her cocooned. She felt warm, safe, cared for. Her eyes drifted close as her hand danced over his thick, muscular chest. She reached out and her fingers tiptoed over his wing. When she caressed the area between skin and wing, he shuddered. Her eyes fluttered open, he gazed down at her with an unbridled look of desire.

Sunlight streamed through an opening in the curtains, beams bounced off the crimson of his wing. She watched, fascinated.

Checking the clock beside her bed, she noted it was well after midday. She didn't want to move. She loved being snuggled against her man. His scent, the hard contours of his body, all left her wanting him more. His heartbeat pounded beneath her cheek, he may be a Demon, but he was hers.

Glass breaking, and shouts from the perimeter of her home shattered their peace. Decimus catapulted from the bed, his muscles rippling with apprehension. "Stay here."

He pulled a pair of jeans onto his naked body and dashed to the front room.

Eve sat up in bed. Her heart thundered against her ribs. She had a feeling of doom deep in her belly. Disobeying, she rose and followed him to the living room.

Outside the broken window, an angry mob was gathered, shouting and yelling. Mrs. Hobbs' voice was unmistakable. "Demons do not belong here. Repent, whore, or get out."

Other shouts followed, directed at her.

"Sinner."

"Whore."

"Slut."

"Murdering Demon."

The cries were deafening. The mob grew restless for blood. Objects thumped against the outer walls of her home, cheers followed. Eve was terrified and snuck a quick glance. Placards with bible passages bobbed up and down as people chanted.

The local minister held a bible above his head and recited the Lord's Prayer.

"Bigots, all of them." Tears slipped over her cheeks.

Decimus slipped up and gathered her into his arms "I think I should leave. I'm sorry I have brought this angry mob to your home."

She swiped at her tears. "No. You are here because I want you here. I will not allow them to dictate who I can and cannot have in my own home." She placed a hand on his chest and stood on tiptoes to kiss him.

She hurried back to her room and slipped into a pair of jeans and a shirt before heading toward the front door.

Decimus had been keeping watch at the window and as she reached for the handle of the door he shouted. "Get back." He raced toward her.

The windows at the side of the door exploded in a shower of glass as planks of wood were catapulted into her house. Loud cheers erupted.

Eve cowered behind the door in fear. She heard the sloshing of liquid and an overpowering smell of petrol reached her nose.

"Decimus." She peered through tear sodden eyes as he swept her into his arms.

"We have to get out of here, baby." He heard the sound of a match being ignited and raced for the back of the house.

Eve heard the minister chanting as she was carried away from the mob. "May the Lord forgive us for our sins. We shall not let evil abide in our community, and those who do not repent shall be cast out."

She heard a *whoosh* as the petrol ignited and her home caught alight. "Decimus, put me down." Eve screamed and struggled in his grip.

"I can't, baby. We have to leave now."

She turned back to see flames licking their way through her home. As they rushed through the kitchen, she grabbed her handbag from the back of a dining chair.

Decimus burst from the house and scanned the yard, unsure how to safely escape the angry mob. Several were coming over the fence, he roared in anger and they backed away.

The situation had turned deadly and she shouted. "The shed, get to the shed."

Decimus ran toward an old metal shed and kicked the door in. He hurried inside, weaving his wings through the doorway before lowering Eve to the ground. Decimus pulled the dented door closed, grabbed a crowbar and jammed it in place to keep the door shut.

Eve was pulling at a large, dusty cover. "Help me." Decimus grabbed the cover and ripped it from the object it hid.

A classic car was revealed. A black, V8 supercharged Holden HQ with the name - *Black Magic* scrawled across the top of the front quarter panels.

Eve raced to a cupboard at the back of the shed. Several beeps were heard as she opened a small, hidden safe.

The jingling of keys drew Decimus' attention to her as she unlocked the car.

"It was my brother's baby. He had two, this was his second baby." She unlocked the door and slid behind the wheel. Thumps pounded the steel sides of the shed followed by shouts. The noise was drowned out as Eve turned the key and the engine rumbled to life. Decimus jumped into the passenger seat, pulling his trailing wings in before closing the door.

"What happened to the first one?" Decimus was impressed with the immaculately restored interior of the car.

"He was killed in it." Her voice was soft and he barely heard her over the roar of the engine.

He chose to avoid the subject for now. "How do we get out of here?"

"Hold on." She pushed a button on the keychain which dangled from the ignition. "I have this covered, I hope."

Exhaust fumes thickened the air but then, the back wall of the shed lifted upward and inward toward the roof. A door he hadn't noticed before. Sunlight streamed in to reveal a back alley. She put the car into gear and eased the beast out into the alley, turning the wheel sharply to negotiate the tight corner.

Eve accelerated down the alley leaving the shouts of anger in their wake. When she peered into the rear vision mirror, she saw the flames which leapt from her home into the sky.

The minister and Mrs. Hobbs stood at the end of the alley but Eve made no attempt to hit the brakes and they were forced to jump out of her way.

"We will find you Demon whore." The minister shouted as she sped past.

"Fuck."

"What's wrong?" Decimus sounded concerned.

"They're going for their cars to follow us." She slammed her foot hard on the pedal and *Black Magic* roared to life. The engine hadn't been started in a month, and Eve knew the car lived for an open throttle. At least that's what Sam had claimed when he had finished working on her. He had crashed his first love - *Red Devil,* at an amateur stock drag-racing competition. The beautifully restored Mustang had been destroyed and her brother's life lost.

She banished thoughts of her brother's demise from her mind as she concentrated on getting away safely. A quick glance in the mirror revealed, she had four cars pursuing her.

"We have to get out of the city." Her hands trembled on the steering wheel.

Decimus placed his hand on her shoulder. "We'll be all right, baby. I have faith you will keep both of us safe."

Eve smiled. "Right. It was people's belief in faith and all the crap that goes with it that has us in this mess to begin with. If we can get onto the freeway, we should be ok. I know a place where we can go. Hopefully, no-one will think to look for us there."

She drove hard and fast through the streets. Winding her way past parked cars and flying past children who played in their front yards.

Finally they hit the freeway and she floored the pedal. The car flew along the road with no regard for the speed limit. Traffic was sparse, police even more so these days. There was no worry about being caught as they sped away from the angry lynch mob.

Chapter Seven

A few hours later, they had left the city well and truly behind. Eve had slowed to a safer speed as they wound their way along country roads.

The sky was a myriad of pinks and purples as the sun set on an exhausting day. A sign heralded a town up ahead.

She glanced at the fuel gauge and noted it was dangerously low. "I have to pull in, we need fuel and I'm exhausted."

Decimus nodded. "I need to stretch. My ass is sore and my body aches from being cramped up for so long.

Eve pulled in to a service station and as the wheels depressed a pressure sensor, a bell rang for service. She eased up beside a bowser, killed the engine and popped the fuel cap. The engine ticked as it wound down. She slipped from the car, lifted the nozzle and started refuelling.

Decimus peeled himself from the vehicle. His magnificent muscles rippled as he twisted and stretched. His wings shook and floated up and down.

Her attention was drawn back to the pump when the nozzle clicked off indicating the tank had been filled. Eve noted the price and sighed. *Black Magic* was a thirsty bitch. But, she had helped them to escape.

Eve dragged her tired limbs into the shop to pay for the fuel. She added food and drinks to the bill. A news report on the television overhead caught her attention but, before she could focus Decimus slid up behind her

"We need to go." He grasped her arm, gave the clerk a searing glare and escorted her back to the car. He turned to see the clerk glance up at the TV and reach for the phone. They climbed into the car and hurried away.

Eve pulled into the parking lot of a small country motel with a flickering neon sign above. They left the car and Eve checked in, giving a false name, while Decimus waited in the shadows.

The room was small; the bed barely big enough for the two of them. Eve sighed and dropped her handbag onto a small bench. Thanks to their fleeting escape, they had no spare clothes.

She dropped onto the bed and lowered her head in her hands. Sobs wracked her body as she wept. Her shoulders shuddering.

Decimus crouched before her. His hands rested on her waist while his wings wrapped around her protectively. I'm here, sweetheart." His voice was soothing, comforting. He placed his fingers under her chin and tilted her head back. He ran his thumb gently over her lips and dabbed at her tears.

"My house." Agony shone from her eyes.

His heart wept for her. "Your life. That is what truly matters. A house, possessions, material things can all be replaced. They are nothing compared to what I have."

"What?"

"You, baby." He leaned in and captured her lips with his own in a moment of passion. "I have you."

Eve drew him to her, laying them both down. Her hands gripped his shoulders, a leg entwined with his thigh. Their lips crashed back together.

They were desperate for each other and clothes were peeled from their bodies, discarded onto the floor. Naked, they melded into a passionate embrace.

His thick, hard erection pressed against her soft belly. Her nipples pebbled and peaked as his hands caressed them. She moaned into his mouth and ground herself against his crotch. Desire built between them, urging them forward. Her heart soared in the warm embrace of her Demon. She would never let this man go.

She gazed up at him as he straddled her body. Their eyes locked, love ricocheted back and forth. Tears welled in her eyes as his filled with pure adulation for her. She had no doubt, he would move Heaven, Earth and Hell to protect her. To ensure she was his for eternity.

#

Sated, spent, following fervent lovemaking, they lay entwined in each other's arms. Their peaceful slumber, rudely interrupted by loud rapping at the door.

Eve sprang from the bed and dressed. She flung open the door to the livid face of the manager.

"You have five minutes to get out of that room and off my property."

"Excuse me?"

"You heard me, whore. Five minutes and then I'm calling the police."

Eve slammed the door without replying. She rushed to rouse Decimus from the bed.

He was already awake and pulling his clothes on. His mood could only be described as disgruntled. "You paid for the damn room, fucking bigot. How did he even know I was here?" He continued to scowl and grumble as he slipped into his shoes.

They left the room and strode to the car. Eve climbed in behind the wheel while Decimus folded himself into the passenger seat. The manager glowered at them from the office window as they drove past.

Decimus reclined in the passenger seat. He didn't complain about the discomfort she knew he must feel with his wings folded in so awkwardly.

She flicked the radio on, *Highway to Hell* blasted out at them. She hurriedly turned the dial silencing the din.

Decimus chuckled. "That song was appropriate for our situation, don't you think?" He kissed her shoulder.

Eve laughed. "I guess so." She flicked the dial and turned up the volume again.

Takin' everythin' in my stride
Don't need reason
Don't need rhyme
Ain't nothin' that I'd rather do

Goin' down

Party time

My friends are gonna be there too

I'm on the highway to Hell

On the highway to Hell

Highway to Hell

I'm on the highway to Hell.

She sang at the top of her voice as she drove through the pre-dawn light toward the freeway.

Eve knew something was wrong. "What the fuck?" Four hours had passed when the steering wheel grew heavy in her hands. It vibrated out of control. The gauges read fine but there was a thumping sound from the side of the car. "Fuck, flat tire." She pulled onto the verge.

She stepped from the car and inspected the tire at the front. It was flat. "Shit." She kicked the deflated front tire. She moved toward the rear in search of the spare. "Fuck. When are we gonna catch a break?" The back tire was also flat. Shining heads of multiple nails were embedded in the black rubber of both tires.

"Guess we're walking. I hope you don't mind roughing it because it's going to take us a couple of days to get to my old home on foot."

Decimus folded her into his arms. "As long as I'm with you, I don't mind *roughing it.*" He winked cheekily.

Eve laughed and playfully slapped his bare shoulder. "Cheeky bugger."

He dragged her closer before kissing her passionately.

She reluctantly broke the kiss when she felt his cock thicken. Now was not the time for amorous behaviour.

"Come on, lover. We need to move *Black Magic* off the road so no one steals her. There's an old truck at the house we can use to tow her back."

Eve climbed behind the wheel, flashed up the motor and eased the car behind a small thicket of bushes. Satisfied it was out of sight, she grabbed her purse and what little supplies they had left, before locking the vehicle.

Decimus removed the heavier bag containing their drinks and took her hand. He raised his wing and shielded her from the sun's heat. She leaned into him and he relaxed. Removing his hand from hers, he wrapped it protectively around her shoulders.

"Wouldn't it be quicker to fly?"

He smiled. "We prefer not to fly, we have had a few incidents with humans and shotguns. Demons and Angels aren't as immortal as people believe."

"So, you don't fly at all?"

"Not unless it's an emergency. It makes humans nervous to see us flying."

Eve snuggled against him. "I understand but I'd love to fly with you one day." She had long harboured a desire to fly with either a Demon or Angel.

"Perhaps one day, I will take you to the clouds." He sealed his promise with a kiss to her temple. "But, for now I am more comfortable with walking beside you."

Eve smiled as they continued to her childhood home.

Chapter Eight

Dusk descended on the western horizon. After walking all day, Eve was footsore and limping. Decimus offered to carry her until they found a place to rest but, she declined, knowing he must be tired also.

"No, I can walk. There's a little abandoned church a short distance from here. We should be able to shelter there for the night."

Storm clouds rose menacingly above them as they continued on. Thunder echoed from away in the distance and the wind blew a gale.

"Hopefully the place won't crumble around me when I enter." His voice was serious but his eyes twinkled with mischief.

"I think they deconsecrate them when they're abandoned so you should be safe. She stood on tiptoe and kissed his neck.

His body shook and, grabbing his arm, she stopped and turned him toward her. "Are you ok?"

Decimus' erupted in laughter.

"What's so funny?"

"Demon's don't cause churches to crumble, consecrated or otherwise. I was pulling your leg." He glanced at the sky. "Rain is coming." He lifted his arm and pointed above at the exact time the heavens opened. Sheets of heavy rain poured down upon them.

Eve glimpsed the small church in the distance before turning to Decimus. "Run?"

Nodding, he swept her into his arms. His black wings folded around them offering protection from the rain. His legs pumped, speeding them both towards their destination.

Decimus leapt over the steel, chain-link fence and rushed to the cover of the entry arch of the church. He set Eve onto her feet and she jiggled the door. Locked.

"Damn." She slammed her hands onto her waist and glanced around for something that may help them to enter.

He moved in front of her and rammed his shoulder against the door. It gave with a sound of protesting splinters as the lock fell away. It swung open revealing the church's interior. Dust motes danced in the air above the pews. Dim slivers of light shone through the stained glass windows causing patterns to reflect from the floor.

Decimus scanned the interior. "Not exactly cosy, but at least we'll be warm and dry."

"After the war, most people fled to the cities – safety in numbers. The farming communities died as homes, businesses and churches were abandoned." She placed her bag on the nearest pew. The church was warm and she did feel safe with Decimus by her side. Driving rain hammered the tin roof above them.

As he sauntered toward the front of the church, Decimus noted a painting of Jesus, his hand raised in benevolence, behind the pulpit. An enormous crucifix was fixed to the wall, off to one side. He frowned, below were blankets neatly folded in a pile. Black and white feathers were sprinkled around.

"Eve, I don't think we are the only ones here." Before he could continue, air exploded from his lungs. The force of the attack slammed him against a brick wall.

Eve screamed as an Angel pummelled her love while he lay dazed on the floor. Decimus recovered and roared his indignation at such treatment. He flung his attacker clear. A loud crunch, the splintering of a pew and a grunt followed.

Decimus struggled to his feet, still a little stunned.

His wings rose above him, he moved toward the figure who lay in the centre of a now shattered pew. White feathered wings protruded from the wreckage, booted feet visible as they hung over the broken back of the pew.

Decimus breathed heavily as he glared at the injured Angel before him. "Who are you?" His fists clenched. "Tell me thy name, Angel, so I may know who I am ending."

Eve hurried to her man and grabbed his tensely muscled arm. "No." Piercing blue angel eyes gazed at her. "You can't kill him, you're not that kind of person anymore."

Decimus' face contorted in rage and he snarled, unwilling to allow his attacker to go free.

She placed a soft hand to his chest. His heart thumped furiously beneath her trembling hands. "Please, honey. Leave it be."

Eve gently led him away from the Angel. She seated him in one of the pews at the back and handed him a bottle of water.

"I'll be right back. Please, stay calm." She kissed his cheek and caressed his cheek with her fingers. "Everything will be fine."

Reluctantly, he nodded. He broke the cap off the water bottle and gulped. When the redness of anger had subsided and his face returned to normal color, Eve grabbed another bottle of water and headed to the Angel. She helped him to sit. He groaned loudly.

"Are you okay?" She held the bottle of water toward him.

Blue eyes stared up at her. "Your *friend* needs to learn temperance."

"You attacked him first."

"A Demon standing before a holy crucifix is offensive to my kind. My instincts took over."

On hearing the Angel, Decimus shouted in disgust. "As did mine, asshole."

"Decimus." Eve growled before kneeling beside the injured Angel. "What's your name?"

"Thomas." He removed the lid from the water and drank thirstily.

"I'm Eve. The man you attacked is my lover, Decimus." She watched as Thomas plucked the pew splinters from his torso, tossing them away like spent matches.

"What are you doing here?"

"This is my church. I am the Patron Angel of all you see." He waved his arm around. "Every dust bunny and church mouse included."

"But, this church has been de-consecrated." A flash of lightning caused her to flinch.

"I am still the Patron Angel, even if there are no parishioners to guide." He brushed the last splinters from his body as he stood. "So what brings you here?"

She recounted what had transpired during the past couple of days and the reason they had sought shelter in the church.

Decimus glared at the Angel while Eve spoke. This was his arch enemy and his lady was speaking to him. Caring about him. It took all his control not to rush over and wrap his hands around his throat.

She finally rose and padded back to him. He noted she was no longer limping. Sitting beside him, she snuggled into the warmth of his chest. "Thomas said we are welcome to stay the night." She brushed her fingers over his chest and felt the stutter of his heartbeat.

He pulled her close, a wing curled around her. She spoke softly about her conversation with Thomas.

Decimus glanced toward the Angel who had been watching them closely. There was something about this creature from heaven that didn't make sense. Shadows marred the tops of his wings. There wouldn't be much sleep in this church.

#

Sunlight caressing Eve's face woke her. She stretched and placed a kiss on Decimus' lips, he was awake and gazing fondly at her. Thomas was also awake. They shared tough strips of beef jerky for breakfast before she excused herself and headed to the back of the church where the outhouse was located.

When she returned inside, Decimus and Thomas stood glaring at each other. It was like a Mexican stand-off. Tension vibrated from both of them. She sighed loudly as she approached the two warriors. "Break it up, there's been enough destruction. The war is over and you two need to learn to get along."

The tense Demon growled softly at the Angel before him.

Thomas turned to Eve. "My dear, why are you with this…. this, poor excuse for a Demon? You are much too good; your heart is too pure to be with such an abomination."

"Regardless of what you believe, Decimus is a good man. He has saved my life, and my virtue, on three occasions. Apart from that, the decision about who I choose to be with is mine, no-one else's."

Decimus smirked at Thomas, stepped beside Eve and wrapped his arms around her. "Come, beautiful. We need to leave, I was never one for sermons and holier than thou attitudes."

Thomas refused to give up. "Be warned, he will corrupt you. Your immortal soul will be forever chained in the bowels of Hell to be tortured for eternity."

"Where the hell do you get this stuff. No-one is going to torture Eve or her soul."

She gazed into her lover's eyes. "I don't mind being corrupted and tortured as long as I'm with you."

He hugged her close and kissed the top of her head.

Eve felt safe in his protective embrace. "If you need us, we are a few farms over, the old McIntyre place. Thanks for allowing us to shelter here. If there is anything you need, you know where to find us."

Thomas smiled. "You have a warm heart, Eve. Maybe you will make an Angel out of your Demon."

Decimus stiffened but before he could turn on Thomas again, Eve said goodbye and led him away.

Chapter Nine

An hour and a half later, they reached her childhood home. Eve sighed with relief. Sad memories about her parent's deaths surfaced, she had lost both within six months of each other. Although they had both lost their fights to cancer, she believed her father had also died of a broken heart. He had loved her mother to distraction, she had been his entire life.

Eve and her brother had not been able to bring themselves to sell the farm where they had grown up. Instead, they visited often to ensure it remained intact. They had hoped, one of them would eventually find their soul mate, and raise their own family here. The surrounding few hundred acres were leased to neighbours and stock roamed the land.

She gathered her man's hand and led him to the back door. Reaching up to a rafter overhead, she located the spare key and unlocked the door to the kitchen.

The farmhouse was old and floorboards creaked underfoot as they entered the darkened room. Eve pushed open the drapes, light streamed in.

Decimus glanced around the room. A small dining table sat by the window where the drapes had been opened. The kitchen housed an old cast iron wood stove, beside it stood a more modern electric one. He wondered which Eve preferred to prepare meals on.

"I'll switch on the solar. It powers the house during the day and charges the batteries we use overnight. She flicked a switch and lights flickered to life along with the fridge.

Decimus stood with his arms crossed and watched as she flitted about.

"We'll have hot water in about three hours." She opened a door and walked into a cupboard. When she turned, her arms were filled with a tin of baked beans and other baking requirements.

"Baked beans on homemade bread for dinner. I know it's not much but we usually bring supplies with us. We don't keep a lot here so as to discourage mice." She placed a mixing bowl and bread tin on the wide bench.

Decimus settled himself on a stool and watched as she prepared the bread. He was mesmerized watching her as she mixed the dough and kneaded it. Flour dust wafted upward, coating her pretty face. Decimus erupted in deep belly laughter when she punched a well in the centre and flour exploded over her.

"Funny, huh?" She threw a handful of flour at him, it coated his dark hair and wings.

Getting into the spirit, he grabbed a fistful of the dry mixture and flung it back at her. It coated her clothes and her hair.

She laughed, grabbed another handful, and leapt from behind the bench. She raised her hand into the air.

His smile became devilishly playful. "Be careful, pretty girl. You may get more than you bargain for if you throw that."

"Is that a threat or a promise?" Her face lit up with a beautiful smile as he stalked toward her. She released the handful of flour.

It covered his face causing him to sputter and cough for a moment or two. "Right, you asked for it." He lunged and swept her into his arms. She squealed with laughter. "Bedroom?"

Eve shook her head, refusing to tell him.

His hands tickled her mercilessly, she kicked and squealed against her much stronger captor. "Okay, okay. I give up" She pointed to a small hallway which led from the kitchen. He carried her through the house until she indicated the master bedroom door.

He pushed the door wide with his foot and placed her onto the bed.

She gazed at him. His touch delighted and aroused her. She wanted him desperately. If the huge bulge in his pants was any indication, he wanted her just as much.

Leaning over her, he ran his hands up her thighs to the fastenings of her jeans. He plucked at the buttons revealing her see through lace panties. He growled from deep in his chest, slid the jeans and panties from her body and discarded them onto the floor. Her shirt and bra followed quickly.

He stood, drinking in her magnificent beauty. In a matter of moments, his own clothes were discarded.

Eve's eyes devoured every inch of his spectacular frame before locking with his.

Decimus climbed onto the bed and lowered himself over her. "You are perfect. I will never let you go." His lips crashed down on hers. Soft moans filled the air as their tongues duelled and tangled. His cock rubbed against her soft folds, as she became wetter, he became harder.

Withdrawing from her lips, he dove onto her beaded nipple. Sucking, nipping then, blowing a soft breath of air across the hard tip. It was excruciatingly arousing. He moved to the other nipple, not wishing to ignore it, and afforded it the same treatment.

Eve lifted her hips, wanting – no, needing, to get closer. She wanted to climb inside his skin and experience every cell.

Decimus moaned, his cock so hard it was aching. Cum leaked from the tip as he savoured every inch of his woman's body. He slid down, kissing, nipping, until his goal was reached.

Eve spread her legs wider, inviting him in. But, no, he lowered his mouth to her folds and sucked. She bucked beneath him as his fingers delved inside with his tongue. His teeth captured her already swollen, over-sensitive clit.

She couldn't take any more. With her fingers firmly wrapped in his hair, her orgasm exploded. She screamed his name as he relentlessly continued to devour her.

Decimus sensed when Eve descended from her orgasm. She became quiet, her body trembled. Lifting himself, he captured her lips and slid home, deep inside the woman he was coming to love.

The velvety softness of her interior wrapped around him like a sensuous glove. He pulled out and slid back into the depths. They fell into rhythm. His hard balls slapped her ass as their lovemaking became frenzied.

"Eve." Decimus arched his back and his hot seed spewed forth.

She gripped him tightly as he pulled her over the edge. They milked every last drop from each other before falling back onto the bed. Decimus rolled beside her, holding her tightly against him. His wings folded around them.

Eve felt safe and loved in his arms. She wanted to keep him forever. She would keep him forever; of that she was sure.

He pressed a kiss to her forehead and she smiled up at him. Their lips found each other in a gentle, sweet kiss.

Eve pulled him closer, embracing his warmth. She frowned and her head dropped against his chest.

Decimus placed his fingers under her chin and tilted her face to him. "What is causing such a beautiful face to wrinkle in a frown?"

"I'm worried. What am I going to do? My hone in the city is gone, I have no job. Where do we go from here? What do we do?" Tears filled her eyes.

He hugged her closer, his fingers travelled her back, soothing. "We can always live on baked beans and homemade toast, amongst other things." His wiggling eyebrows set her to giggling.

"We need more than that. You're a big man. You need meat, vegetables. What little supplies we have here won't last long. I'll see if Dad's old truck has enough fuel to get into town. I'll check with the agent and find out how much money I have from leasing the land." She sat up and turned to him. "And us?"

He wrapped her in his arms. "We are forever. We are eternal, my love." Decimus kissed the top of her shoulder. "I'll be yours for this life and beyond. I love you."

Eve closed her eyes and smiled as a tear of happiness broke free and trickled down her cheek. She snuggled into him and whispered, "I love you too."

Chapter Ten

Eve removed the bread from the oven, the delicious scent wafted through the house and caused their stomachs to grumble in anticipation of their feast.

Decimus held out two plates but, she shook her head. "I need to slice and toast it first." She nodded to the stove where a pot of baked beans simmered gently. "Can you stir the pot for me, baby?" Removing a knife from the block, she carved the bread into slices.

"The honey pot?" His breath whispered down her neck as he spoke near her ear. His hand slipped between her legs and cupped her pussy. Her legs weakened and she placed her hands on the bench to steady herself.

Her voice was husky. "You can stir that one later. For now, the one on the stove, please."

His lips traced the pulse in her neck, feathering light kisses. "Are you sure?"

"Later. We need to eat."

He growled as he stepped away from her reluctantly and stirred the bubbling, hot beans.

She placed two slices of bread into the toaster and set it.

A few minutes later their dinner was ready and they sat down to eat.

#

They spent the evening cuddled into each other on the old couch. Eve switched on the TV. The screen lit up with the local news.

"Police continue their search for Evelyn Macintyre of South Bridge, today. Neighbours of the young woman said she was kidnapped by a Demon known as, Decimus. After setting fire to her house, he fled the scene with his victim. Neighbours said, despite their efforts they were unable to prevent him from taking her.

A service station attendant reported seeing the couple on Monday night and called police. After a report by this news station, a member of the public also phoned in a sighting. A vehicle registered to Miss Macintyre was found abandoned."

Images of *Black Magic* flashed onto the screen and Eve's heart sank. "Fuck." She sat forward, tears flooded her eyes and she trembled.

Decimus pulled her back into his arms and held her as they listened further.

"This recent incident has reinforced the incompatibility of Demon/human association and Community Leaders have called a halt to all Demon Rehabilitation programs. Stricter controls over the movements of Demons have also been enforced. They are now required to report to their local police station at nine in the morning and evening. They are also to be back at their place of residence no later than ten at night. Failure to observe these new laws will result in penalties being imposed."

Eve glanced at Decimus, his face was set in a frown. "Do they really believe they can hold Demons in their flimsy prisons?"

"I don't know but this report is bullshit. You didn't kidnap me. The neighbours were the ones who threatened my life and burnt down my home."

The report continued. *"Decimus is also wanted over an incident involving the partner of Miss Macintyre. He is accused of causing grievous bodily harm. Mr Jacob*

Eve switched off the television in disgust and wrapped her arms around Decimus. He trembled with rage.

"Nobody knows where we are, baby. We'll be safe."

He wrapped her in his arms. "How are you going to go into town for money and supplies without being recognized?"

"Fuck. Dad's truck is registered to me and the agent will have to know it's me if I'm to get money for supplies. Fuck." Eve dragged her fingers over her scalp. "What if we go to the police and tell them the truth?"

He shook his head. "They would never believe you. I'm a Demon, they would say you are under my influence. If we attempted to approach them, I'd be shot on sight and they would take you away from me. I can't allow that to happen. I won't lose you."

A loud knock at the front door startled them. They looked at each other. "Who the hell could it be at this time of night. I didn't hear a car or see headlights." Eve stood and padded to the front door. Decimus followed.

She unbolted the door and opened it gingerly before throwing it wide. "Thomas. Why are you here?"

The Angel stood nervously glancing around. "I heard you two might be in some trouble. I thought maybe I could help in some way."

Eve stepped back inside. "Come in."

Decimus stood behind her protectively, his hand on her shoulder.

"Are you hungry?" she asked.

Decimus didn't wait for the Angel's answer. "What the fuck can you do to help us?"

Eve glared at her man. "Come and sit down. I'll make you something to eat while we talk."

Eve started off. Thomas stood back. "You first. I don't trust that easily."

"It should be I who does not trust you, Angel. After all you did attack me first."

"You were in my church, it was an affront to both God and myself." Knowing one of them had to give in, he pushed past Decimus and strode down the hall, following the direction Eve had headed in.

She glanced up as they strode into the kitchen.

Thomas sat at the table. Decimus sat opposite where he could keep a close watch on his natural enemy.

Eve set a jug of water and glasses in front of them and sat.

Thomas poured himself some water and gulped a large mouthful. "You need supplies, don't you?"

"Yes. Before this mess I was going to pick them up in town tomorrow."

"I'm well known in town, I can go and get them for you and find out if they have any idea this is where you are."

"Inform the police, you mean." Decimus growled.

Thomas glared at him. "If I informed the police, they would lock you up and throw away the key. Not, that I would mind but, I won't have Eve's heart broken."

"Thank you, Thomas. Now, are you hungry?" Eve asked the previously unanswered question again.

"Yes, I am. I would appreciate something to eat."

Eve stood and headed to the pantry. She removed more beans and the freshly baked bread. "Decimus, would you like more?"

"Yes, please." Decimus glowered at Thomas while the sound of plates being pulled from cupboards filled the room.

After a few minutes, she set a plateful of toasted bread and hot beans before the men.

Thomas thanked her and began eating. "Write down a list of everything you need and I'll get them for you."

Both men finished their meals and she took the plates to the sink. "You're welcome to stay here with us, Thomas. It's the least we can do after your kind offer."

Decimus scowled but remained silent.

"I'll make a bed up for you in one of the spare rooms." She ran a hand over her jealous Demon's abs as she passed. When their eyes met, she winked. A promise of what was to come.

Once she was out of sight, Decimus moved quickly. He slammed his hands on the table before Thomas and leaned over him. "If you betray her, I will kill you."

Thomas smirked. "Jealousy does not become you, Demon. I would never harm Eve." He stood. "You should be more concerned about what your former comrades are up to. Demons from the city have suddenly gone to ground. Something is going on with them." He strode from the kitchen.

Decimus stared after him, concern etched on his face.

Chapter Eleven

The deafening flapping of wings woke Decimus in the small hours of the morning. It was not the sound of any bird of the night. He rolled over and looked out the window at the half-moon as it set

Moving Eve from his chest, he rose from the bed. Their lovemaking had been quiet, but no less ardent, and she was exhausted.

He smirked as he pulled on a pair of pants. He was certain he had seen a flash of white feathers through the slightly open door as he licked Eve's pussy. One large hand had clamped over her sweet, seductive mouth muffling her cries of rapture as she came. Thomas had been enjoying a voyeuristic view through the gap in the door. *Filthy Angel.*

He padded to the kitchen. The sound of rustling feathers and heavy footsteps on the old wooden porch alerted him. He sensed more than one was outside, be they friend or foe was still to be decided.

He drew a carving knife from the block Eve had used earlier. It was a poor excuse for a weapon, he would have given anything to have his sword. Unfortunately, it was back in Demonville along with his armour. He and his fellow Demons had hidden their secret cache in case Lucifer returned. As the months on Earth dragged on relentlessly, their leader's return looked more and more unlikely.

He pondered, if Lucifer returned and demanded he resume his duty as a Battle Demon, would he give up what he had now?

He opened the door inch by inch. "Decimus," his old comrade whispered.

He threw the door open. "Severus. What are you doing here?" He stepped from the house after closing the door. Taking his old friend by the arm, he moved them away to where an old corrugated tank stood.

"Marius sends his greetings, and invites you to return to your people. He is pleased with the chaos you have caused the humans." Severus grinned. "Marius wants you to take your place by his side as his first general. He is building an army to take over the Earth, just as Lucifer wanted."

Severus gripped Decimus' shoulder. "Think of it, all the women you can fuck, their souls enslaved for eternity. The power, my brother. The delightful sins we can enjoy." He shook Decimus' shoulder for emphasis.

Decimus shook his head. "I cannot return. I have everything I want right here. Please, tell Marius I appreciate the offer but I can't be his general. I want a peaceful life with Eve."

Severus' face darkened with disbelief. "You would refuse your King, the King of all Demons on Earth?" His brow furrowed. "You walk a dangerous line my friend, you would do well to reconsider. I will give you one night to think on it. I will return tomorrow, until then I have others to call to our King's side." Severus open his wings and launched himself into the air. "Until tomorrow night." The words were barely heard as he rose into the sky.

Other Demons launched themselves into the air, following their leader.

Decimus remained in the cool of the night. Crouched down, his mind going over all he had been told.

Marius, one of Lucifer's most unstable lieutenants, had named himself King. He had to be stopped or this was not going to end well for the humans.

Decimus sighed, he didn't want any part of what was going on. He wanted to spend the rest of what mortal life was allotted to him with the woman he loved. He was a changed Demon. Others would call him pussy-whipped, but he knew in his heart, she had redeemed him.

He sighed and looked up at the sky, hoping for guidance but knowing it might never come. He turned and walked back into the house.

He climbed in beside Eve and watched as her serene face smiled unconsciously at his return. Wrapping her in his arms, he drew her to him. His lips pressed against her forehead. The scent of her hair familiar and comforting.

Sleep would not return to him tonight.

#

The next night, he found Severus waiting for him by the tank. He was smoking a cigarette and blowing rings as he exhaled. Two other Demons in full battle armour flanked him, their demeanour was guarded. The Demon beamed at him. "Are you ready to go Decimus?"

"My answer is still no. I cannot, and will not, do what Marius asks. I have a life here and I won't give it up."

Severus turned nasty. "You aren't free; you know. The humans could find you at any time. The police could be tipped off at any time. Even without a friendly tip-off, how long will it be before they come for you? We found you easy enough. Be sensible, come with us."

Decimus scowled at Severus.

"Marius will bring you into the fold one way or another. If you don't come now, he will send me back for you. I will be accompanied by many more Demons. Incurring his wrath will be damaging for both you and your whore." He turned and flicked the cigarette away.

When he turned back, his face met with Decimus' fist. A loud crunch sounded as the bones of his nose shattered. Blood spattered his chest.

"Don't you *ever* call Eve a whore!" Decimus hissed with anger.

The guards stepped toward Decimus. Severus raised one hand to stop them while the other covered his broken and bloodied nose. "You, my friend, have been pussy-whipped into submission. You are not thinking clearly. Consider yourself warned. I will return." He launched with his guards into the dark sky.

#

Eve rolled out dough for the day's bread, and when she glanced up, Thomas smiled. She loved cooking for the men. They remained tense around each other, but Thomas brushed it off when she asked him about it. Decimus was also quiet on the matter which annoyed her somewhat. She needed him to be open and honest with her.

Her lover was quiet, reserved about something. She knew he was hiding something. But, *if he thinks it of importance that I know, I'm sure he'll tell me, she* reasoned.

She left the dough to rise and joined Decimus in fixing the chicken coop. Thomas had headed to town to purchase laying hens. A new garden bed for vegetables had been prepared, and Eve was adamant they would be able to live off what they grew. Only meat and foodstuffs they couldn't grow would need to be bought.

Thomas was always happy to go into town. He seemed eager to distance himself from the dark glares Decimus threw at him. Eve was thankful for the Angel's help. They had managed to stay off the radar for more than a week.

Chapter Twelve

Eve perused the furrows of earth. Her hands were covered in the black soil which would nourish and nurture the seeds they intended to plant. Decimus and Thomas were working on a fence near the back of the property while she finished setting up the vegetable patch. She smiled with satisfaction and brushed the excess dirt from her hands. When she turned, she found herself face to face with a Demon in black battle armour.

"Hello, Eve, I believe?" Severus gave her a sickly smile which caused her stomach to drop through the core of the earth.

"Who are you?" She stepped back from the large Demon.

"I'm Severus, a friend of Decimus." He smiled again,

Eve's skin crawled with disgust, the little hairs on her arms stood on end.

"He's out on the farm fixing a fence. Do, do you… do you want me to go find him?" She backed up another step, her heart rate rising to near panic levels.

Severus shook his head with a chuckle that turned her blood to ice. She *really* didn't like this guy, everything about him screamed danger.

"What do you want?" She took yet another step backwards.

"I have a friend of yours who would love to see you again. No need to pack. We'll take you straight to him."

Alarm bells rang. "I don't have any other friends who are Demons, Mr. Severus. I have a lot of work to do here. Good day."

The Demon was not taking no for an answer. He advanced, she retreated until hard armour pressed against her back and strong hands gripped her arms. She twisted her head to find another large Demon behind her. His face grim and set.

"Ah, my dear Eve." Severus ran his hand down the side of her face. She winced and pulled away. "Did I say you had a choice?" He smiled as he bound and gagged her with strips of material. "Let's go, he's waiting."

Eve struggled uselessly against her bonds. She screamed in vain as she was picked up and launched into the air, the Demon's black wings unfurling for flight. Her struggling ceased, fear of falling overriding her fear of being kidnapped by two Demons. Her farm dropped down as they rose. Her heart hammered in her chest faster than she had ever thought possible.

Fuck. Decimus, help me! Her thoughts screamed out to her lover, but she knew she couldn't reach him through thought alone.

Severus glided, his wings outstretched, catching the small thermals as they sped over the countryside. Hours passed before Eve saw the dark silhouette of the city against the pinks, reds and oranges of the setting sun.

A short time later, they landed on top of one of the more exclusive hotels in the city. Demons standing guard on the roof allowed them to enter.

Something had changed, the mood of the city was different. There were no cars and none of the expected city noise. Something had happened. It was darker, and she sensed, more dangerous than she could ever have thought possible.

Severus dragged her down two flights of steps before knocking on the door to a penthouse. A guard opened it and eyed her in the grip of her captor. He grunted and nodded, allowing them entry.

Eve's eyes were downcast and her shoulders slumped. From what she had seen, there was no chance of her slipping the guards and escaping. Her mind drifted back to the farm, and the warmth of Decimus' love. She hoped he had figured out what had happened to her and was on his way. But, she despaired. What could one Demon do against the mass of guards who were here?

She was catapulted forward into the penthouse. Standing in front of the windows, a tall Demon stood with his back to her, his wings relaxed. The gag was removed from her mouth and she worked the stiffness from her jaw

"Ahh, my dearest Eve, so good of you to accept my kind offer and join me."

Eve's heart stuttered as she recognised his voice.

"Marius." Her voice was barely a whisper. Memories of their last encounter flooded back - *I will have women chained at my throne for my pleasure. I think you'd like that, to be my sex slave, chained and collared waiting to do my bidding.* His words had chilled her back then, now they set her blood to ice.

He turned and smiled at her. "I see you remember me." He padded toward her, reached out and traced a calloused finger across her jawline. "I have missed your sweet face in the office. It's been too long since I saw you last, and my heart does pine for a fine woman such as yourself."

She wrenched her face from his hand. "I'm sure there are plenty of Demon-fans out there who would be willing to fall at your feet. I am not one of them."

Marius shook his head before leaning close to her ear. "But, my sweet Eve, there are none I would like to slam against the wall and fuck until she can't walk."

Eve shuddered with revulsion. Marius' tongue slid along her jaw. She recoiled away from him.

His laugh set her on edge and caused her to tremble.

He held her firmly with one hand while he ran the other down her neck and over her collarbone. "Such a tasty morsel, one to be savoured. I can see why Decimus took such a shine to you."

She forcibly turned her head away from him.

He tilted her head and touched his lips to hers before pushing her into the arms of one of his lackeys. "Take her, get her cleaned up and prepared for me. I'll be down in the throne room. Until later, my dear."

She tried to squirm from the iron grip of the Demon guard.

Marius strode from the penthouse with Severus. She was left with four guards. They pushed her into a nearby bathroom. A bubble bath awaited her. She was ordered to strip and get in. The guards made no effort to leave.

"Privacy?"

The Demons scowled and snarled. Three of them left. It was obvious the fourth was going nowhere.

Eve turned away and shed her clothes. She slipped into the huge tub and sank below the fragrant bubbles. Her stomach churned with fear as she tried to relax.

"Hurry up."

She had almost forgotten the Demon was there. Almost. She washed quickly, stepped from the tub and reached for a large, fluffy towel. She dried herself off and as she wrapped one towel around her body her hair in another, she noted the guard watching her.

He grunted as he pointed to a counter where there were several sheer teddies.

"Demon of few words, aren't you?"

She picked up a black teddy and held it out. "What the fuck." The garment was nothing more than a bunch of strategically, and not-so-strategically tied strings. It was one of the skimpiest undergarments she had ever laid eyes on. "I am not wearing this or anything like it."

"Fine, King Marius won't mind you naked."

Eve cast a scathing look at the Demon whose lips curled into a smile. He was obviously picturing her naked or with next to nothing on. Her venomous glare seemed to have no effect on him.

She knew this was a battle she couldn't win so she selected the demurest teddy available. The accompanying panties were thongs in various colours. She swallowed her fear and allowed anger to slowly replace it.

She slipped the deep blue silk-and-lace teddy over her body and pulled on a thong which matched.

When she turned, she didn't miss the twinkle, and lust, in the guard's eyes. If his cock was aroused, it was well concealed by the armour. He shuddered and it scared her to know he was struggling to maintain control.

She shook her hair from the towel and rubbed it as dry as she could. A brush was placed on the counter and she ran it shakily through her hair eliminating the knots.

When he decided she was done, the guard grabbed her arm roughly and dragged her from the bathroom into the penthouse. The other three guards formed a ring around her and escorted her downstairs to the ballroom.

Her breathing quickened in fear as they entered a foyer. Men, bloodied and beaten, were chained to the walls. Some groaned and shifted, trying to find comfort, others were still. Heads hung in defeat, or death. A strong odour of blood, faeces and urine hung in the air. Eve tried not to gag.

Chapter Thirteen.

Eve was pushed toward two large, golden handled doors. Two Demons flung them open and she was accompanied in the previously beautiful ballroom. Her step faltered and she stumbled as she was pushed in the back toward the throne where Marius reposed.

The throne, set on a raised dais, was composed of human skulls. Empty eye sockets and grinning jaws mocked her. Her eyes perused the three wretched women who were chained at Marius' feet. Her eyes flicked up to the Demon.

He sat casually, a leg thrown over the armrest of the large chair. She shuddered when her eyes noted the huge bulge in his pants. He watched her closely as she approached, one hand stroking the dark hair of a quietly sobbing woman at his feet.

Intense fear rose in her. She was powerless to keep it at bay. Her mouth dried and her body trembled as she was pushed before Marius and forced to her knees. The cold wooden parquetry was hard on her kneecaps and she yelped with the shock. Her eyes dropped to examine the floor, preferable to looking at Marius. She heard the tapping of steps as her captor descended toward her.

He ran a hand through her hair, gripped a fistful and pulled her head back to meet his lusty gaze. "My dear, you are positively fuckable."

"I don't belong to you, I belong to Decimus. He'll kill you if you lay a hand on me." Her voice broke as she spoke her beloveds name.

Marius laughed. "He'll be here soon, pet. You are my leverage and, if he fails, my prize." He tugged viciously at her hair.

She squealed as her scalp erupted in burning pain. She bounced to her feet to lessen the sting. Marius dragged her to where a mannequin stood. A set of Demon armour was displayed awaiting its rightful owner.

Marius pulled her tight against him, the sharp planes of his armour biting into her flesh. His hand wrapped around the curve of her breast and he twisted her nipple through the thin material of the teddy.

Eve desperately tried to squirm away from the bastard's hand but, he squeezed the soft flesh again, causing her to squeal in discomfort.

He shook her. "Take a good look. This is Decimus' armour, he wore it proudly into battle. My beloved brother in arms. We fought side-by-side. When our Prince of Darkness abandoned us, we suffered together. We sought comfort in fucking as many women as we could drag to our beds." He laughed maniacally, before turning and placing a kiss to her temple.

Eve shuddered in disgust. His hand continued to fondle her breast. She struggled against him.

He dragged her to a weapons rack and pointed out a large black sword with red edging. "This sword, also belongs to Decimus." Marius ran a fingertip over the blade, a smear of blood left behind. He pulled the digit away and inspected the cut. Blood seeped from the small wound. He turned and smeared it over Eve's lips while holding her head tightly in place. "Taste me, my sweet. Taste the power you will soon be tied to. Decimus will find another woman to warm his bed."

The metallic taste and scent of his blood made her sick to her stomach. She gagged as she fought the urge to vomit. She lobbed a ball of spit at his face, it landed with a satisfactory splat on his nose.

Marius blinked in surprise and smiled. He wiped the spittle away from his face and sucked it into his mouth with his fingers. "I'm sure there are other parts of you that taste much more divine. But, I see you need to learn respect." His face darkened as he lifted his hand and struck her face hard. She crumpled to the floor.

Hot fire erupted across her cheek. Eve's sobbing joined that of the other women.

The monster crouched down beside her.

"I do not wish to mark you, or damage you so you need to learn to respect and obey me. I want you whole, healthy and wanting me. Decimus may have you back if he succumbs to my will and does my bidding. But, I *will* have your body before he gets you back *–if* I decide to give you back"

Marius reached for something behind him. Eve noticed another set of boots behind the self-proclaimed Demon King, a guard. There was the clink of chains and the scent of soft leather. Marius dragged her up by the hair and back to his throne. He pushed her to a sitting position on the opposite side to the other women and caressed her soft throat.

Tears fell as he placed the collar around her neck and tightened it. He attached the chain to the collar and rose.

"There, beautiful. you are now where you belong."

#

"Hold it while I tighten the wire." Decimus' muscles shone with sweat as they bulged with the effort of using the wire tensioner.

Thomas obliged, holding the wooden fence post in place while Decimus worked.

Grabbing a hammer, Decimus secured the taut wire to the post. "There's something I've been wanting to ask you for a while now.".

"Yes?" Thomas secured the next line against the post.

"When we met, you were alone in a church that had been abandoned."

Thomas straightened. "You want to know why an Angel who should have had a place as an active church's patron, and been loved by the parishioners, was alone and living in an abandoned church."

"Yes." Decimus released the tensioning tool from the tight wire of the fence.

"I fell."

"You fell?"

"Yes. After the great battle, and the loss of our Lord, many of us became unstable. I went to a very bad place." Thomas gazed over the farmland. "I was given a position at a church a few towns over. I was their Patron. I was fine at first, and I thought things were going to be okay. But then, the minister's daughter, she…" Thomas looked away, embarrassed.

"She seduced you?" Decimus couldn't keep the surprise from his voice.

"It wasn't hard to fall under her spell. She was a beautiful young woman, very much like her mother." Thomas sighed. "It was only a few days after the final battle. I was weak. My mind wasn't healthy. I should have resisted them, told the wife to stay faithful to her husband, the daughter to save herself for the one she truly loved."

"You,… you slept with her mother too?"

"Pleasures of the flesh can drive any man or Angel to sin." Thomas reached behind him and plucked a black feather from his perfect white wings. He held it up. "Every so often one of these shows up. A reminder of how close I was, or still am, to completely falling."

"You've not completed the cycle of the seven?" Decimus cut and coiled the wire that was left over.

"No. There was Lust, in the women I bedded from the parish. I would use their bible studies' groups and single sessions to sleep with them. Envy, for those men whose women had resisted me. My Pride was the thought that I could get any woman into my bed, and I often did." Thomas packed away the tools they had used to fix the fence. His face clouded with dark memories. "I found Greed in wanting more women at one time, and Gluttony in the reality. I never imagined any woman would find themselves attracted to me. The fact so many did, stroked my ego."

"It's the wings, chicks dig the wings." Decimus watched as Thomas's wings and shoulders slumped in defeat.

"I was almost consumed by Wrath. When the men of the town and parish found out what I had been doing, sleeping with their wives and adult daughters…." Thomas paused. "I,… I drew my sword when they came for me, the woman in my bed was killed, but not by my hand. She was the daughter of the town's mayor. He was the first to die by my hand, in my grief and anger for the death of the girl in my bed. I did not stop until I was covered in their blood. Three men lay dead or dying, not sure how many were injured. I ran, I had to. I don't know how I can gain my redemption from this, my time of sin, my falling."

Decimus placed a hand on his shoulder. "You have not fallen completely yet, Thomas. There is hope for redemption, but to find it for the deaths of three men." He sighed. "I'm no Angel, I'm a Demon, I don't know much about redemption, Sin yes, but not that." Decimus thought for a moment. "I know someone once said, *Love is the great Redeemer, With Love, all can be forgiven.*'"

"Who said that?" Thomas picked up the box of tools and they headed back to the farmhouse.

"An Angel I once knew." Decimus smiled as they walked.

A flutter of wings from behind brought them to a stop.

"What a delightful couple you two make." Severus smirked as two other demons landed behind him.

Decimus frowned. "Why are you here? I have told you, I am not interested in joining Marius' insane plan to enslave the human race. It is doomed to failure."

Severus clucked his tongue. "My dear Decimus, I was sent to give you a message. Someone who means a great deal to you is being entertained at Marius' fortress. Of course, if you don't want to come and get her, I'm sure Marius will understand. It's so easy to find another human to fuck. He is quite taken with her so, he will not be disappointed. He has already expressed the desire to be pleasured by her."

Thomas restrained Decimus as the Demon's muscles bunched for attack.

Severus ignored the threat. "You have one day to come to Marius' palace, also known as the Grande Hotel."

"I thought you said it was a fortress?" Thomas held a struggling Decimus tight in the circle of his strong arms.

"It is, there are a large number of our former comrades who have rallied to his call for dominance over the pitiful humans." Severus looked Thomas up and down. "There may be a place for one who has almost fallen completely, you should consider joining us. Sin is much more satisfying than Piety."

Thomas snarled is displeasure.

"Suit yourself. We'll expect you soon, Decimus." Severus launched himself into the sky with his guards.

Thomas released his new friend. "What will you do?"

"I will go and get my woman back, and kill the bastard who has her."

"I'll go with you." Thomas had been affected by Eve's kindness and friendship. There was nothing he wouldn't do to help her.

Decimus appreciated the fact Thomas wanted to help and he nodded. "If we get her back, I will be forever indebted to you."

"I'm doing this for Eve." Thomas prepared himself by stretching his wings.

Decimus also stretched his to their limits. A grimace crossed his face. It had been far too long since they had been used for their intended purpose.

Thomas noticed his friend's grimace of discomfort. "Been a while?" He flapped his gently.

"What?"

"Been a while since you took to the skies?" Thomas rested his hands on his hips as he gazed upward and felt the warm sun on his wings.

"Yeah, I don't normally fly. But, I'm gonna have to reconsider. Damn cars are so uncomfortable." He spread his wings, the crimson sheen on his black feathers catching the glorious rays of the sun. They shimmered, giving off an ethereal glow. His body warmed as the sun kissed his wings. His heart feared for his love but, he had no doubt they would be together again. And, soon. He stretched his wings fully again, tested them with a couple of flaps and launched himself skyward. "Come on asshole, Eve doesn't have all day to be rescued."

Thomas launched into the sky and caught up with Decimus in no time.

Chapter Fourteen

Both Demon and Angel soared toward, urgency spurring then on as fast as their wings could take them. Thomas moved alongside Decimus as they approached the church where they had first met. "I need to get something from down there." He pointed toward the ground. "It may help you to defeat Marius." He banked and descended

Decimus followed, impatient with the delay.

Thomas landed, pushed the door open and hurried into the darkness.

Decimus followed and watched as the Angel hurried to a small storeroom and collected his silver and gold armour, and his sword. He dressed quickly and checked his blade. He returned back to the room and brought out something wrapped in a deep indigo cloth. "This is what may turn the tide in the battle." He unwrapped the object, Decimus' breath caught.

"How, why? Where did you get it?" He was afraid to reach out and touch it.

Thomas sighed. "I fell, remember? It was given to me to help achieve my redemption. I was charged with a mission, to redeem as many Demons as I was able. Those I could not redeem; I was to destroy" Thomas glanced at the blade in his hand. "I will not use it, so I must find another way to redeem my sins."

Decimus placed a hand on Thomas' armoured shoulder. "If I can help you to find a way to your redemption, I will do so."

The Angel nodded his thanks. "Let's go, we can't lose any more time, Eve needs us."

#

Eve sat curled up on the floor beside one of the other weeping women. Marius had moved them all to the dining hall, led by their chains, humiliation and despair burned deep within her heart. Her face was swollen, and no doubt bruised, where Marius had hit her. It throbbed in time with her heartbeat. Her shoulders slumped and she despaired about being rescued from this Hell on Earth.

Marius reached down and dragged her up by one arm to settle on his lap while he ate his meal. He brought a fork full of roast pork and gravy to her lips.

She turned away, refusing, despite the protesting grumble of her empty stomach.

"Eat, or I will force it down your throat." His tone was harsh and brooked no refusal.

She opened her mouth and he pushed the food in. "Now close that pretty mouth and chew."

Closing her mouth, she chewed slowly. He leaned forward and licked a spot of gravy from the corner of her mouth and she flinched. The food tasted like ash and she resisted the temptation to spit it back at his face.

"That's my girl. Now, swallow." He nuzzled her throat.

Eve fought the nausea as she sat uncomfortably in his lap. The bulge of his desire poked the cleft of her ass, fear rushed through her.

A guard approached Marius and whispered into his ear. The word, Decimus, reached her ears and her heart skipped a beat. She tensed in Marius' lap. His hand stroked her back, sending shivers of hatred and abhorrence for him through her body.

"Ah, my pet, looks like your lover has arrived to take his place as my general. Soon, very soon, I will hold this pathetic world and its souls in my grip." He turned her to face him. "And, you will be by my side. I will have you, hmm, perhaps while he watches." He drew her close and kissed her, his teeth gripping her bottom lip and pulling on the soft flesh. His tongue swiped at the captured lip before he released her.

Eve glared at her captor and gagged. She had no doubt, he was deranged, maniacal. Lust and desire burned his eyes. She shuddered as he ground his erection against her bare ass.

"Come. We should not be rude and keep Decimus waiting." He rose with her in his arms. As he slid her down his body and onto her feet, he groped her breasts and ass. Ignoring the other women, he fisted her chain and they left the dining hall.

Eve stumbled behind the cruel Demon as he dragged her through the hotel. Twice she fell to her knees but he refused to stop, instead pulling her along the rough floor until she could once again rise to her feet. Her knees were grazed, battered and bleeding. Tears cascaded over her cheeks.

At the main entrance to the ballroom, he stopped and handed her chain to a guard. She was pulled around to a side door. Out of sight.

#

Decimus and Thomas stood in the ballroom surrounded by four guards. While they waited for Marius, they took the opportunity to observe their surroundings. The macabre sight of bloodstained human skulls the throne was perched on, showed the damage that Marius had already inflicted.

The Demons now ruled this city, and several others had also fallen if rumours were to be believed. It was a blow to humankind.

Marius appeared and approached them. A smile on his face, and his arms spread wide in welcome.

"Decimus, my brother, you have arrived. I see you have brought a friend. Curious, the pets you keep, my brother." He continued smiling as he took his place on the throne.

"I'm only here for Eve. Return her and we'll be on our way without harming you." Decimus glanced around. "Where is she?"

Marius laughed. "Are you threatening me?"

"Take it as you will. Where is she?"

Marius sighed and beckoned toward one of the guards who stood near a side door.

Marius bristled with rage as his beloved was led toward Marius. He noted her state of undress, what she wore left nothing to the imagination. His beautiful woman was on display for everyone to see.

Marius was handed her chain, he tugged and she fell face down across his lap.

"As you can see, she is perfectly fine." Marius ran his hands over the soft globes of her ass.

"Take your hands off her." Decimus burned with anger, His fists clenched by his side.

"She will not be harmed, unless you choose to disobey me." Marius slid his fingers between her ass cheeks and Eve cried out in distress.

His love's cry shattered Decimus' heart. "What would you have me do?" He sounded defeated, even to his own ears.

Thomas snapped his eyes to his friend. "You're not going to try to release her? Are you telling me, you are content to leave her in the hands of this monster?"

Marius ignored Thomas' protest. "Take up your sword in my name. Fight by my side. I will give you an army of Demons to command and a city to rule." He caressed Eve's ass with long strokes as she sobbed.

Decimus was overcome with rage which was barely controllable. His body trembled, his knuckles turned white and his nails bit into the flesh of his palms.

"I might even allow you to have your woman but first, I will savour my prize." He smiled as he pinched her ass cheeks hard. Eve screamed with the pain.

Decimus' heart was breaking. "Very well." He bowed his head to his new master.

Eve sobbed loudly. "Please, no."

"Quiet, my pet, the men are speaking." Marius slapped her ass bringing another scream from her lips.

"I have taken the liberty of having your armour and sword prepared for you, in anticipation of your return." He indicated to the set of armour and the large blade which stood ready.

Decimus crossed the floor and examined his armour. He stripped to his underwear, donned the armour and took up his sword. It felt like a lost limb had been returned to him. The grip and weight familiar in his hand.

Eve now sat upright on his enemy's lap. Decimus noted her watching him with a mixture of fear, sadness and uncertainty. Fury blinded him at the sight of the ugly, dark bruise which marred her beautiful face. He gripped his sword tightly, resisting the urge to step forward and slice through Marius' neck.

"If I may make a request, my Lord?" He raised the tip of his sword.

"Ask. If it is within my power to grant, I shall do so." Marius stroked his hands down Eve's arms.

"May I give my beloved a kiss, to assure her I will return triumphant?" Decimus dropped to one knee.

"Of course, loyalty should be rewarded, as should your devotion to your woman." Marius set Eve onto her and feet and rose. He pushed her toward Decimus.

Decimus caught her in his arms and tilted her face with the tips of his fingers under her chin. Her eyes glistened with fear, her body trembled. A single tear dripped down her cheek and she bit her bottom lip in an effort to hold back her sobs.

"Hush, sweetheart." Decimus caressed her face, his fingertips tracing the dark bruise on her face. He pressed his lips against hers, his wings folded around her. "Be ready to run to Thomas," he whispered.

Eve gazed at him, she was beginning to understand, she nodded.

"Remember, no matter what happens, I love you." He kissed her again, spun her around and pushed her toward Thomas. She rushed to the Angel and he gathered her into his arms. His white wings enfolded her.

Decimus turned back to Marius, his sword drawn and ready

Marius watched with disbelief as his greatest warrior, and best hope for the complete domination of the human race, defied him.

"This plan of yours is insanity, I will not fight for you, ever. I will however, fight for Eve." He levelled his sword at his enemy.

"So this is how you choose to serve your King? You will be slaughtered and your woman will be mine for the rest of eternity." Marius shook his head. "I thought you were smarter than this. you surprise me with your foolishness." He drew his own blade and charged.

Eve watched the battle from the safety of Thomas' arms.

Marius raised his blade over his head and brought it down hard, the ring of metal clashing against metal as Decimus raised his sword in defence. Sparks cascaded to the floor as their blades clashed.

Thomas noted the approaching guards. He held Eve tight and drew his own sword. He held it outstretched, protecting her as they backed away. "We have to get out of here. Decimus wants you safe." He whispered to her as he eased her back with him.

"No." She turned toward the sounds of grunts and clashing of swords.

Marius' onslaught against the man she loved, was furious, savage. His muscles strained with the force he exerted, trying to disarm and slay his former ally.

She struggled to free herself from Thomas, his arms tightened around her, holding her in place as he stepped back "Let me go. I can't leave him." She wept, tears rolled down her face.

"Thomas, get her out of here." Decimus shouted as sword nicked Marius' shoulder.

Marius retaliated. His steel glancing off Decimus' armour.

The two Demons exchanged blows, equally matched, parrying and grunting as they struggled for supremacy. Decimus drove Marius toward the dais. The Demon King stumbled backward, falling to the floor, his sword thrust up in defence. Decimus raised his sword over his head to strike.

Marius kicked out at Decimus, knocking the Battle Demon off balance. His sword fell from his hand and slid over the floor. Marius sprang to his feet and attacked, his sword slashing at Decimus.

Decimus rose to his feet, lunged for his sword and raised it to defend himself. He swung and knocked the Demon King's sword from his grip.

Marius growled and threw himself at Decimus. Decimus' own sword flew from his grip and clattered to the floor. Their bodies rolled and slid across the parquet floor, shattering a glass display case.

Thomas hurried Eve from the ballroom as shattered glass showered in every direction. He levelled his sword at any Demon who dared to approach them.

Eve struggled and shouted. "Please, let me go to him."

"You can't help him." Thomas dragged her to safety. The sound of clashing swords and grunts of pain slowly faded as they hurried away.

Thomas hurried through the hotel, pushed through the entry doors and, hugging Eve tight against him, launched into the air.

Eve screamed in despair at abandoning the man she loved deeply. It tore at the Angel's heart but he had promised Decimus, he would keep her safe. He rose higher into the air and headed back to the farm.

Decimus' exposed body glistened with sweat. Rivulets of blood flowed from cuts inflicted by Marius' sword and broken glass. Shards of glass caught in his shoulder length hair and a large piece was lodged in his shoulder. He used the pain of his injuries to focus his anger. used to the burning pain to feed his power.

He felt at ease knowing Eve was safe with Thomas. Many of the Demons Marius used as guards were not Battle Demons. They were juniors, 'sword fodder' who feared confrontation with Angels. They would make no attempt to reclaim his love.

Marius slid across the floor and recovered his sword.

Decimus raced to where his sword lay. He rolled to the floor, recovered his weapon and sprang back to his feet. His hand grasped the handle, his fingers caressed the familiar leather.

Marius charged, the blade of his sword shone under the lights of the chandeliers.

Decimus readied himself for the attack.

Both men were evenly matched. Both had been commanders of Hell's armies and hand-picked by Lucifer to lead groups of Demonic soldiers in the battle for Earth and the souls he'd intended to claim.

Decimus' thoughts distracted him for a mere fraction of a second, enough for Marius' blade to slice through his cheek. The skin burst open, nerves exposed to the air. His face burned with pain.

Marius' eye lit up with delight at having inflicted injury on his enemy. He regrouped for another assault.

Decimus was ready this time and drew back his blade. Marius stalked him, overconfident with his small victory. It was to be the beginning of his downfall.

Decimus put all his weight behind the force of his swing. The blade connected with Marius' arm which held his sword. It sliced through muscle and bone at the base of the shoulder, not protected by armour, and the limb dropped from his body.

Marius howled in pain as blood pulsed from the open, and bloody, stump. His eyes glowed red and he snarled at his adversary. His wings spread wide in attack formation, he reached for his sword, prying it from the fingers of the fallen limb. "You have gone too far. I will now ensure you are kept alive long enough to watch me take your female. Then, each of my men will take their fill. She will never have a moment when she is not on her back with a Demon deep within her. And, from where you will be chained on the wall, you will watch." He hefted his sword and shoulder charged Decimus, knocking him to the ground. His sword again skittering from reach.

The stench of Marius' blood filled Decimus' nostrils as his enemy dropped to his knees and pinned him down. "I *will* find her and the Angel and they will both pay."

Decimus growled and when his arm thrust upward, the silver bladed dagger, which Thomas had given him, was revealed. He stabbed at the self-appointed King's neck.

Marius felt the searing pain of the blessed dagger and his body stiffened as pain flowed through his body. His eyes turned to Decimus. "Blessed dagger." Life drained from him and he crumpled to the floor his last breath left his lungs.

Decimus grunted as his enemy fell atop him.

Demon guards watched in stunned silence as Decimus shoved Marius from him and jumped to his feet. He leaned over to corpse of the Demon King and pulled the blessed blade from his neck. Blood spattered the floor. The guards dropped to their knees before Decimus and watched as he raised his sword and sliced the head from Marius' body. He picked up the head of his enemy and held it high as he spoke.

"Marius is dead. Release the humans from slavery and return to your rightful places. No other Demon shall claim this city as theirs." He tossed the severed head to the feet of the guards.

"Lord Decimus…" one Demon spoke, ignoring the open eyed stare of the severed head at his feet.

Decimus raised his hand. "I am not your Lord; please, do as I ask." He retrieved his sword from the floor and sheathed it. "I'm a Demon, no different to you."

He strode from the hotel. He took a moment to bask in the sun as it bathed his battered wings in warmth. He sucked in a deep breath and launched himself into the sky.

\#

Eve paced the church where Thomas had brought her. The pew where Decimus had thrown Thomas, remained broken. The Angel had not yet removed it.

"Why am I here? Why am I not at the farm? Will Decimus know we are here?" She had asked the questions repeatedly, her mind not thinking clearly.

Thomas had explained earlier; the church was the safest place for her. Demons normally avoided them. She had wept in his arms and pounded her fists against his chest. She'd begged for him to return her to Decimus but he'd refused to give in. Her mood changed from anger to grief and back again as she paced impatiently.

Thomas would not give in to the grief stricken woman no matter how hard it was to refuse her. Both he and Decimus were united in their need to keep Eve safe. He would never admit it to her, or Decimus, but he felt deeply for the beautiful woman he had held in his arms. His heart broke when he realized, she would not be his redeemer.

Unable to prevent her from pacing, Thomas had retreated to a private corner of the church where he normally slept. Lifting the bedding, he withdrew an old tobacco tin he had found. Within it lay his shameful secret.

He opened the tin and thoughts of his disgrace filled his thoughts as he studied the feathers within. The first black feathers had appeared in his wings a few months before.

His sins had finally caught up with him. Each time he found one in his wing, he plucked it and added it to the tin.

A noise outside, drew his attention away from the tin. He closed it and slid it back under his bedding.

Eve glanced at him, stopping mid stride in her continuous pacing. She had heard the noise also. He rose to his feet and drew his sword.

"Wait here," He commanded as he brushed past her.

He moved to the door and quietly opened it the barest of fractions. Seconds later, his eyes widened and he flung the door back.

Decimus stood before him. Bloodied, battered, his shoulders sagged and his body shook with exhaustion. An open gash on his face seeped blood, angry and raw.

Eve screamed his name as she sprinted toward him and threw herself into his arms. She cried hard against his armoured chest, bloodied hands stroked her dark hair, his lips pressed kisses to the top of her head.

"Hush, sweetheart. It's over." His voice was soothing but tired.

Eve pulled back and peered up at him. Her eyes glistened with a mixture of hope and fear. "It is?"

Decimus gave her a weary smile. "Yes, Marius is dead. Killed by my own hand." He glanced at Thomas who stood back allowing them to soak in the joy of their reunion. "Thanks to Thomas, it's over. He gifted me with a blade which had been blessed. It's known as a *Demonslayer*. A sacred dagger Archangels wield in battle against Demons." He caressed her face with his fingers and wiped away her tears with his thumb.

"Let's go home." Eve was eager to return to her home.

Thomas stepped forward. "Is that a good idea? Won't the other Demons hunt you down?"

Decimus shook his head. "No, the others are returning to their lives as before. I don't know how the humans will react to this change. Marius and his cohorts held many humans as prisoners. Many in the city perished from the cruelty unleashed on them. I don't know how they will again live in peace."

"You have done your best, my love. It is not for you to worry about."

He lifted Eve into his arms. "Let's return to the farm, I need to rest, and hold you in my arms where I know you are safe." He lowered his head and kissed her lips gently.

She caressed his face, careful to avoid the open wound on his cheek.

"Thomas, you will return with us?" Decimus asked as he carried Eve to the door.

"I would like to very much."

They stepped from the church. Hugging Eve close, Decimus launched into the sky. Thomas launched a moment later after closing the door.

Chapter Sixteen

Eve rolled from her man's arms with a grunt as Decimus crashed to ground at the farm. His breathing was ragged, he lay moaning as the pain of his injuries and the effort of flying, overwhelmed him.

Thomas landed beside them and helped Eve to her feet. They rushed to Decimus and helped him to sit before easing him onto his unsteady feet.

Decimus winced as Thomas jammed his shoulder beneath his injured arm. Eve supported his other side and, together they helped the injured warrior into the farmhouse.

Eve unlocked the door and pushed it open. Thomas half carried Decimus in. "I'll run a bath and we'll get you cleaned up and into bed." She glanced to Thomas. "Can you help him out of his armour?"

She locked the door behind them, not fully convinced yet that they were safe and hurried to the bathroom. She leaned over the bath, jammed in the plug and turned the taps on. She watched as the tub began to fill with hot water before crouching and opening the cupboard beneath the sink. She retrieved the first aid kit, antiseptic and bandages. A sound at the door drew her attention. Thomas, still in full armour, supported a beautifully naked Decimus wavering beside him.

"I figured you'd want more than just his armour off for his bath." Thomas smiled.

"Yes, thank you."

Thomas helped Decimus limp to the bath where Eve took hold of his arm. "Let's get you in the bath, baby. I'll clean you up and get your wounds dressed, then we can get you into bed to rest."

Decimus groaned as pain shot through his body. He stepped into the bath with their help. His aches and stiff muscles were soothed by the hot water as he slid beneath it. The antiseptic solution she poured into the water stung his wounds and he cursed.

Eve picked up a washcloth and began to cleaning away the blood and dirt.

He winced as shards of glass were pushed deeper into his skin.

Eve frowned when she noticed the glistening shards. "Fuck. I'll get the tweezers and remove the glass. Baby, I'm so sorry I was hurting you." She kissed his lips.

He lay his head back and closed his eyes as she rose and grabbed the tweezers from a shelf in the cabinet. She dipped them in a capful of antiseptic solution and began the arduous job of removing the shards from his flesh.

Decimus winced, his breath coming in strained gasps with each shard she pulled out. There were many more pieces lodged in his flesh than he had first thought. When she was finally satisfied, all glass had been removed, she returned to cleaning her exhausted lover. His body trembled as she thoroughly cleaned every inch of him.

The bath water had turned a ruddy pink with the mixture of blood, sweat and antiseptic.

Decimus protested when it was time for him to leave the comfort of the warm water. Thomas and Eve helped him to his feet and over the lip of the bath. The Angel held him firmly while Eve towelled him dry. He was then lowered into a chair.

He sat meekly while Eve ministered to his numerous wounds. With bandages covering his arms and legs, and a plaster covering the gash on his face, he was bundled into bed.

Eve padded to the kitchen and started their dinner. It was then she realized, she was still wearing the sheer teddy. She hurried to her room and changed. When she returned to the kitchen, she flung the disgusting lingerie into the trash and went back to preparing their meal.

Thomas sat at the table as she made their dinner. He spoke softly, a touch of pain in his voice. "I'm going to have to leave you when Decimus is recovered enough to be able to protect you again."

Eve looked up from slicing potatoes. "What? Why?" She placed the knife down, wiped her hands on the apron she wore and stepped toward him.

"It's complicated."

"It can't be that complicated, you have to live somewhere so why not here?"

"Trust me, it is and I can't stay."

Eve sat on a chair beside him. She gathered his hand in hers, caressing his knuckles with her fingertips. "You can tell me, it's okay."

"I'm…" Thomas blushed, and turned away. "There's a woman I know. She is one of the kindest and most beautiful souls I have ever met. I am an Angel, almost fallen. I did some terrible things after the war. I seek redemption, and Decimus seems to think I can find it with the love of a good woman. But the one I love…" he paused, feeling the pain in his heart grow in her presence.

"Loves another." Eve finished for him.

He watched as understanding dawned on her face. She reached up and caressed his face, brushing aside golden locks and tucking them behind his ear.

"You see my problem."

"I do. What will you do?"

Before he could answer, his body tensed. Still clad in his armour, he got to his feet and drew his sword. "Stay here, lock the door behind me."

He hurried to the door while Eve raced to the window. She heard the distinctive fluttering of wings, too large to belong to a bird. Peering through the window, she watched in horror as several Demons landed on the back porch and a dozen others were landed in the back yard. "Fuck."

Thomas stepped through the door and confronted the Demons, sword drawn.

Fear pounded in Eve's chest as she watched Thomas approach the Demon closest to the house. They spoke briefly before Thomas returned. She opened the door.

"They have asked to see Decimus."

Eve shook with fear for the man she loved. "Why? He's got nothing to do with them anymore. You heard him say, he left them behind." She glanced from Thomas to the gathered Demons.

"I'll see them." Decimus' voice was weak and he leaned against the wall for support.

Eve spun around and frowned at how pale and sickly he appeared. "You should be in bed." She hurried to his side.

"I'll be fine." He leaned over to kiss her. "I need to allow them to see me. I am still one of them even if I don't think like them or belong with them anymore."

She understood how he felt and helped him to the door. His movements were stiff but he held his back straight, head high and his wings pulled back. Like the proud and strong man, he was.

Eve's heart overflowed with love as she helped him outside to meet the Demons.

"Decimus." The Demon who appeared to be leader greeted him.

"Octavius." Decimus returned the greeting and they shook hands. "What brings you and your men to my home?"

"We come to ask a boon of the Demon who ended the madness of Marius. Severus attempted to take over where Marius left off. I'm afraid we took exception, and he was torn apart, wings first."

Decimus and Thomas both winced, knowing it was the most painful and shameful way for a Demon or an Angel to die. Decimus locked his arm around Eve and pulled her close. She leaned gently against him, circling his waist with her arm. Supporting him with her love.

Octavius indicated the Demons behind him. "We have come to ask you to lead us. We are without a master and are lost and confused. How are we to survive in this world?

Like you, not all Demons want to continue Lucifer or Marius' insanity."

Eve peered up at Decimus, his face was grim and his eyes showed he was deep in thought. Thomas shifted beside them, uncomfortable with having so many Demons around him.

"You are unable to lead because you fell when you were seduced by a Succubus." Decimus stated the reason for Octavius' fall.

The Demon dropped his eyes to the ground and nodded. "Yes."

"I am no leader, I am not the one you seek." Decimus shook his head.

"But, you are honourable. You came for your woman. You are a better Demon than Marius could have ever been. He would have allowed the woman to be killed and simply taken another." Octavius turned to Eve. "I remember you from the rehabilitation program, you were always kind and helpful to those of us who were in need."

Eve smiled. "What do you need?"

"We have no place. The humans ran those of us they did not kill, from the city. We are the few who remain. We do not hold their actions against them. It was Marius' doing which has caused their hatred and our displacement." Octavius sighed, it was obvious he was weary from their fight and flight from the City.

Decimus was quiet and tense. He looked over the assembled Demons. "How many of you are there?"

"There are twenty-seven who survived, some have minor wounds. Five were left at a small church we found nearby as two have severe injuries. They could only make it that far before they succumbed to exhaustion."

Eve stepped forward, concerned. "How severe are their injuries?"

Decimus' lips twitched. His Eve, always wanting to help those in need.

"A few have deep lacerations; one has a broken arm." Octavius' voice was tight with worry.

"Can you bring them here?" Eve turned to Decimus, seeking his approval. He nodded. She turned back to Octavius. "We can help you, I have a few spare rooms here. We can nurse the injured back to health. It may be a bit cramped until we find a more permanent solution."

Octavius quirked an eyebrow. "Decimus?"

"You heard my lady."

Octavius bowed. "Thank you, we are grateful." He sent Demons to bring the men from the church.

Eve cleared an area in the living and dining rooms and lay out blankets and other makeshift bedding. The two injured would be settled in beds in the spare room.

While they sat at the table drinking coffee, Octavius recounted the story of what had happened after Decimus had left. After killing Severus, the Demons under Octavius, had released the humans who were held prisoner. The humans had retaliated quickly.

Many Demons had been killed or captured. Octavius and his men had fled, flying for hours, before one of them suggested that they seek out Decimus for guidance. The vote had been unanimous and they had begun their exhausted flight towards Eve's farm. They were guided by one of the Demons who had visited before.

Decimus appeared tired as he spoke with Octavius.

Eve and Thomas left them to talk further and set about preparing food for their dinner. The house was ready for the injured Demon's arrival.

Eve placed her hand on her man's and squeezed. "You need rest, baby." She kissed his temple.

"First, we need to discuss what is going on in your pretty little head."

"I want to set up a safe place for Demons to live, a sanctuary of sorts. We can live off the land, grow crops to feed us and sell, raise animals for meat. We can erect some buildings to house them. I have hundreds of acres of land. It can be for any Demon or Angel. She glanced pointedly at Thomas. "Whoever wishes to, can come and live here in peace."

Octavius smiled.

Decimus thought on it for a moment and nodded his head in agreement.

Octavius slapped Decimus' shoulder causing him to wince with the pain. "Then it's settled. I'll have the men help out wherever you need, whenever you need. We will work for our food and lodgings. We will build a community here, safe for Demons *and* Angels." He turned to Thomas. "It might be hard to accept our mortal enemy living amongst us, but if we can live here on Earth amongst humans, I'm sure we can survive amongst Angels as well."

Eve smiled at Thomas before she glanced at Decimus and Octavius. "Decimus and Thomas have gotten along very well, after their first meeting that is." She grinned.

"I have already told Eve I will be leaving." Thomas crossed his arms over his armoured chest.

"Why?" Decimus didn't understand and his eyes narrowed with suspicion.

"It's a personal matter. But, after hearing you speak, I have an idea. In my travels, if I come across a Demon or Angel who wishes to find a place to live peacefully, I will send them to you. I will act as an agent for your sanctuary."

"That is a great idea." Eve kiss Thomas on the cheek, he blushed with embarrassment.

Decimus stifled a yawn as Thomas' new job, seeker of displaced Demons and Angels, was agreed upon.

Eve placed her hands on his shoulders. "I think it is time for you to get to bed." Her breath tickled against his ear. He nodded and tilted his head back, pressing his lips against hers. Eve helped him to his feet.

"I'm going to rest now."

Octavius rose and gripped Decimus' forearm. "Rest well, my brother, we will speak more in the morning."

Eve helped Decimus from the kitchen and into their bedroom. He sank down on the soft mattress with a heavy sigh.

He pulled Eve close. "It seems we have a few houseguests. We are going to have to be quiet until they have built their own places." His eyes glittered with lust, his tiredness suddenly gone. "You should close the door." He kissed her passionately

Eve giggled in his arms and disentangled herself from him. She managed to escape his grip and closed the door, before returning to his wandering hands.

Her body responded to his touches, gasps and moans escaped her lips as her desire for him grew. His hands popped the buttons on her blouse, exposing her lacy bra.

His head dove into her cleavage and he tugged on her nipples through the sheer fabric.

"You need to rest." Her protest was at best, half-hearted.

"Hmm." His voice vibrated against her already hard nipple.

He flipped her onto the bed and rose above her. His wings opened as his mouth ravaged her. He peeled back the bra and her breasts tumbled into his hands. While he nipped and laved at her pebbled mounds, his hand moved down her body to the snap of her jeans. He flicked it open and slid down the zipper. His fingers dived inside her panties and found what he sought. Her folds were wet, welcoming.

Eve gasped as his fingers reached deep inside her. Her swollen clit reacted to every touch, every brush of his fingertips. Her hands reached for the soft spot between shoulder and wing and caressed him gently. He shuddered and she felt his cock harden as it pushed against her belly.

He growled as he stood, tore his pants from his body and reached for her jeans. They were off in a flash and he climbed back onto the bed. He held himself over her. "You are the most beautiful woman I have ever laid eyes on, both in body and soul. I am never letting you go. I love you, more than my life."

His lips crashed onto hers as he slid his cock into her saturated pussy.

Eve writhed below him as he found his pace, pushing ever deeper within her.

Her fingers again moved to the junction between shoulder and wings, her fingers fluttered over the sensitive skin. Decimus moaned, she felt his cock flinch with excitement.

His wings shuddered as Eve's touch stimulated both them and his cock. His balls drew up hard against him as he made love to her harder and faster. They jumped over the edge together, he roaring her name, she screaming his.

Decimus would never tire of his beautiful woman. Together they would build a life he never knew was possible. As they descended, he held her tight and ravaged her lips. I love you. You are my life, my eternity.

"I love you too, baby, with every cell in my body and soul.

A shadow passed by the window as they clung to each other in the fog of their after love.

Thomas shouldered the small bag he had brought with him from the church. He gazed out ahead of him, over the land of the farm. Beyond, lay his new job.

Maybe, his redemption……….

Read on for Chapter one of *Angel's Redemption: Book Two of the Redemption of the Fallen.*

Angel's Redemption: Chapter One

The woman sat on the desk in the small office, her legs crossed provocatively, and her naked upper body hidden behind a large book. She smiled seductively as the object of her seduction entered.

He took one look at her and closed the door.

"Amy..." he said, his voice and the growing bulge in his pants revealing his lust.

"Thomas," Amy said in return.

Amy tossed aside the book, revealing the soft curves of her breasts, nipples budded in the chill of the office. She uncrossed her legs revealing a pussy bare of hair, her eyes on Thomas. She watched his reaction. His breathing quickened as she slipped off the desk and came to him. Her deft hands quickly unbuttoning his shirt. She pressed her soft red lips against the hard pectoral muscles, her tongue teasing his nipple into an erect bud to match her own.

"Are you..." he began, but she hushed him.

"I want this, you want this..." she said, as she lowered her body to his hips and her hands dipped down, unfastening his pants. "Why deny the desire between us?" he groaned as she took his hard cock in her hands and stroked the head with a fingertip. Thomas bit his lip and shuddered in torturous pleasure.

"Jenna told me about the little private 'Bible study' session that the two of you enjoyed the other day." she licked the bead of moisture from the slit at his head. He groaned and his legs trembled. "I was hoping we could come to a similar... Arrangement." she opened her mouth and took him deep, her tongue suckled his length. His moans of pleasure spurring her on.

Soon, Thomas could take no more. With a hoarse roar he came, his seed spurting down the back of Amy's throat. He gripped her blonde hair and pulled her from his cock. She licked her lips, the mere sight sending him hard again. Thomas reached down and lifted the naked woman up, he carried her over to the desk and put her over it, stomach down. He positioned himself behind her, using his feet to spread her legs. She moaned as he entered her.

Warm, wet and welcoming sensations greeted his shaft as he thrust into her. Amy's soft moans gave way to ecstatic cries of pleasure as she moved back into each thrust. Her generous breasts pooling on the polished wood of the desk as he pounded her, gaining speed as his own climax rushed. His wings spread out in all their glory as he came within her with a roar, to be answered by her climaxing scream. Behind him, a jet black feather fluttered to the ground.

#

Thomas bolted upright, his eyes adjusting to the darkness and his cock standing at attention from the dream. It was more of a memory. He wondered what had woken him, when he heard the distinctive high-pitched scream of a woman in distress. He got to his feet and adjusted himself before leaving the safety of the old overpass and headed towards the frantic screams.

Dried grass and dirt crunched beneath his feet as he made steady progress to an abandoned house. The woman's frantic screams echoed through the night as the voices of men joined the noise. He came up quietly to the house where there was a single candle burning in one of the rooms. Shadows danced on the wall through the window. Thomas came up to the glass and peeked in. His blood boiling as he witnessed the scene before him.

A young woman was held down on the filthy floor by three men. Stripped of her clothing, she struggled futilely against them.

"Let me go!" she screamed, her voice hoarse.

"Nah, we'll keep you, have some fun. Right boys?" one of the men said as the others lifted her up onto the table and flipped her onto her stomach. "Oh yes…" said the man as he removed his pants, baring pale white buttocks to the candlelight. "We are going to have some fun with you." His hand reached out and he caressed the woman's ass. She whimpered and kicked out behind her, trying to get him in his crotch, he grabbed her foot and held it up. "Oh I see you're really into this." He said sadistically.

Thomas could not allow these men to violate her. He drew his sword and stepped back.

#

Grace's heart hammered against her chest. Adrenaline and fear coursed through her veins as she struggled against her captors. Her mission to find her sister could not end like this. The Slavers had taken Ebony along with several other girls. It still shocked her that not even a year after the great apocalypse that men had descended into the madness of the world today. There were a few precious cities where the surviving armies of Heaven and Hell had integrated themselves with human society. But there were far more that hadn't.

Humans had gone back to their baser natures in the blink of an eye. Grace and Ebony had been travelling with a group of refugees from one such city. The Demons had taken over their city, and the few small human outposts had been overrun by the Demons. They had enslaved the humans that had not escaped. Grace, Ebony and their travelling companions had been lucky. Until they had come across the small town where the Human slavers were waiting to ambush them.

Grace had gone on ahead to scavenge for supplies, and hadn't heard the screams until it was too late to help. She watched as the slavers rounded up each of the group, Ebony included, and put them all in chains and lengths of rope.

Grace had followed along behind them at a discreet distance, trying to figure out a way to rescue her sister and the others. To her dismay, she realised that they were heading back to their former home, back to the Demons.

She had double backed to the abandoned farmhouse, hoping to find some kind of weapon that she could use against the slavers. Each man had a gun or a baseball or cricket bat or something that could be used as a weapon. Grace had never killed a man before, never met one that deserved to die. Now she had met ten. The three who held her down and were about to violate her, and the other seven who were escorting her sister and travelling companions.

Grace struggled in the firm grip of the bastards who held her face down on the wooden table. The air of the old house musty, but chill on her naked flesh. She could feel the varnished surface of the table sticking to the sweat of fear that coated her skin as she breathed hard and fast. "Let me go!" she had screamed only to be met with their cruel laughter. She fought hard, trying to kick the guy behind her in the jewels, only to have her foot captured and held out behind her.

She felt his hands run over her ass and down along her thigh. She shuddered in revulsion. "Fuck you! You sick fucks! If I ever get free, I'll castrate the lot of you." She said with such force that spittle flew from her lips as she struggled.

Laughter echoed behind her. "I think we'll just have to keep you bound pretty." The man behind her said, his voice dripping with evil promise.

Grace grit her teeth and closed her eyes, they'd take her, but she would fight them every step of the way. She struggled again. Only to have them press harder on her shoulders, pinning her down. The man behind her shushed her, telling her to be quiet and good and it would all be over shortly.

Glass shattered behind her, startling the men with gasps and curses as they drew away from the table. Grunts and shouts erupted with sounds of violence as she rolled off the table. The single candle flickered and went out as it was knocked over. Darkness enveloped the room. Sounds of crashing and screams of pain resounded in the house as her rescuer attacked the men. She crawled blindly, causing one of the men to trip over her as he stumbled around.

Grace found the only exit to the rest of the house and scrambled to it. A hard hand grasped her arm and pulled her against a sweaty chest, and a cold, sharp blade pressed against her throat.

"Move or scream and I'll slit your throat, bitch." The hot rancid breath of her captor caressed her cheek and assailed her nose. The noise in the room and abated to soft groans and someone's death rattle. Her heavy breathing and pounding pulse harsh in her ears as her captor sidled around the room, trying to escape.

A fluttering of wings nearby caused him to jump.

"Move and the bitch gets it!" he said snarling.

Grace held herself perfectly still in his grip. The blade pressed hard against her throat caused a tiny stinging cut against her skin and a small red line appeared, unseen in the darkness.

"Release her, and I will let you go." A voice in the darkness declared. The man behind her scoffed.

"Yeah sure, this bitch here is my insurance policy." He said, holding her tighter and causing her to squeak as the treatment.

"You have only one chance to live." Came the reply from the darkness. The figure moved slightly into the dim light from outside the house. A perfect silhouette of a winged man was outlined in the poor light that came from the window.

"I'll take my chances with the bitch." Her captor replied.

"So be it." The silhouette said.

In a move that defied her eyes, the winged man retreated into the darkness. Her captor laughed nervously as he moved through the house, almost dragging her with him.

"You and I are going to have some fun when we get away from here, sweetheart…" he said, sneering. The blade was still firmly pressed against her neck and she could feel the slight dampness of her own blood slowly trickling down to her collarbone. The metallic scent of her blood in her nose mingled with the lingering scent of his sweat and bad breath.

#

As they moved through the house, he checked every doorway and hall before they got to the entryway. He pulled the knife away long enough to reach for the front door's handle.

A flash of light against metal and a sharp cry from his lips were the only indication that he had been attacked. He pushed her away and reached for something in his belt. Bright flashes of light and an eruption of ear-splitting gunshots resonated through the entryway and echoed through the house. Grace ducked and held her hands over her head as she cowered. The scent of his blood assailed the rest of her senses as her eyes tried to readjust to the darkness of the house and the ringing in her ears lessened.

Her panting breaths cut into the deadly silence as she sought the attacker and the man who had captured her. She gasped and scuttled back as the winged figure stood up, towering over the prone form of her captor. He stepped closer to her and leaned down. Strong arms went about her waist and brought her over his shoulder. Feathers tickled her nose and made her want to sneeze. An action that she held in desperately, not wanting to blow spit and snot over her… Rescuer… or was he going to finish the job that those bastards had started? Grace wasn't even sure if he was an Angel, or worse a Demon.

Grace struggled weakly in his grip. Firm hands going over her naked butt to steady her as he walked with her down the steps of the abandoned house.

"Put… put me down, please!" she begged. The hard metal of his armour was poking her in places that she really did not wish to be poked.

He shifted her and put her down. Grace swayed a little and he put his hands over her arms to hold her steady.

"Are you all right?" he said. His shadowy figure now cast in the dim light of a crescent moon revealed that his wings were white. Grace looked up at him, her eyes in awe of his handsome features.

"Yes, I'm ok, a bit naked and cut but I'm ok." She suddenly felt self-conscious, despite him having had a good eyeful of her nude body. She wrapped her arms around her upper torso, trying to cover her breasts, while she pressed her thighs together in an attempt to cover her privates.

"What's your name?" the Angel asked.

"Grace. What's yours?"

"I'm Thomas." The Angel smiled, and so help her if she didn't almost melt when he did.

*****

Angel's Redemption: Book two of the redemption of the Fallen Series coming soon!

Author's Note:

Thank you so much for reading "Demon's Embrace" I truly hope you enjoyed reading the story of Decimus and Eve. These two are my favourite so far in the Redemption of the Fallen Series. Look out for Thomas' story in Angel's Redemption coming soon!

I'd also like to thank Susan Horsnell for her hard work in editing the revised edition of *Demon's Embrace*. Your tireless work has made this story really pop!

There will be more of the Fallen to be redeemed through the discovery of love, look out for them too!

If you'd like to contact me, you can find me on Facebook. Give me a 'like'

https://www.facebook.com/scarlettjrose

Visit my website:

http://rockincola83.wix.com/scarlettjrose

If there's anything that may seem amiss with the book, a typo or anything that is out of place, please let me know, so it can be fixed up.

www.ingramcontent.com/pod-product-compliance
Lightning Source LLC
Chambersburg PA
CBHW070952120726
47910CB00004B/1208